Pascal Garnier
Pascal Garnier was born in Paris in 1949. The prize-winning author of more than sixty books, he remains a leading figure in contemporary French literature, in the tradition of Georges Simenon. He died in 2010.

Emily Boyce
Emily Boyce is in-house translator at Gallic Books. She has previously translated *Too Close to the Edge*.

Jane Aitken
Jane Aitken is founder of Gallic Books. She has previously translated *The Front Seat Passenger*.

The Eskimo Solution

GALLIC

The Eskimo Solution

Pascal Garnier

Translated from the French by Emily Boyce
and Jane Aitken

Gallic Books
London

A Gallic Book

Original title: *La Solution Esquimau* © Zulma, 2006

English Translation copyright © Gallic Books, 2016

First published in Great Britain in 2016 by

Gallic Books, 59 Ebury Street, London, SW1W 0NZ

A CIP record for this book is available from the British Library

ISBN 978-1-910477-22-9

Typeset in Fournier MT and Calibri by Gallic Books

Printed in the UK by CPI (CR0 4YY)

24681097531

1

Louis had slept on the bottom bunk in the children's room. He was surrounded by soft-toy monsters and a fire engine dug into his back. Somewhere outside a drill ripped into a pavement; it must be daytime. Louis turned over and curled up, knees under his chin, hands between his thighs, nose squashed under a downy pink dinosaur smelling of dribble and curdled milk.

Why had they rowed the previous evening? ... Oh, yes! It was because Alice wanted to be cremated whilst he wanted to be buried. For Alice, with her straightforward common sense, it was crystal clear. First of all, cremation was less expensive; secondly, it was cleaner; thirdly, it avoided uselessly occupying ground (think what could be built instead of the Thiais cemetery, for example!); and fourthly, her somewhat romantic conclusion was that she would like her ashes to be scattered off the coast of Kalymnos (where they had spent their last holiday) from the bow of a beautiful white boat.

He had interrupted her a bit abruptly. First of all, when you're dead you don't give a flying fuck about the burial costs; secondly, we already tip enough muck into the sea; thirdly, cemeteries are much more pleasant to wander through than dormitory towns; and fourthly, given the progress of science, it's entirely possible that one day we'll be able to recreate life from skeletons, whereas a handful of ashes thrown in the sea, well … He'd accompanied the last point with an obscene gesture.

And who was going to pay for his fucking burial? Was it not enough that he sponged off everyone while he was alive, did it have to continue after his death? Such egotism! Would he like chrysanthemums every Hallowe'en as well?

Of course he wanted chrysanthemums! And trees filled with birds, and cats everywhere! Wasn't she the one who went into raptures over the mossy old gravestones in the Père-Lachaise? That one where the stone had split under pressure from a growing laurel tree?

OK, so why didn't he put money aside to pay for his old moss-covered gravestone? Why was that then?

Here we go, money, it's always about money …

After that all he remembered was a sordid slide into a petty domestic squabble and the harsh realities backed up with numbers that she threw in his face. He didn't have the ammunition to argue with Alice about money, so he had risen from the table, saying, 'If that's the way you feel, I just won't die. That'll be cheaper, won't it?'

And that was really what he had in mind. It was a conviction rooted deep inside him: he would never die.

But that certainty had been severely shaken this year; four of his friends had died. Obviously, as he was forty, he had encountered death before, but this was different. Before it had always either been old people – an uncle, an aunt – or acquaintances who weren't expected to live long, or if they were young, accidents, mostly car accidents, and the deaths seemed normal. But the last four had been people like him, going to all the same kinds of places, enjoying the same books, music and films. Their deaths had not been sudden; they had had time to get used to the idea, living with it for months, discussing it calmly, as you might discuss money problems, work problems or problems in your relationship. And it was that attitude of rational acceptance that had thrown Louis. People like him (not exactly like him now they were dead) had accepted the unacceptable. Four in one year.

As for the others ...

Every day at the same time I go up to my study, read over these pages and ask myself, 'What's the point of writing a story I already know off by heart?' I've explained it to so many people that the tiresome formality of putting it down on paper is about as exciting to me as opening the TV guide to discover *The Longest Day* showing on every channel. In an ideal world I'd sell the story as it is, in its raw state, to someone who had some enthusiasm for writing it. Or who didn't, but would write it for me all the same. Not that it's a bad story, far from it. Madame Beck, my editor, is the only one to have expressed any reservations. I had a hell of a time winning her over.

'It's the story of a man in his forties called Louis, who's a nice guy but skint, and kills his mother for the inheritance.'

Madame Beck's harsh-sounding name suits her down to the ground. After a long, sharp intake of breath, she replied.

'Not exactly original.'

'Wait a minute, let me go on. It's a very modest inheritance – but that's beside the point. Since everything goes to plan, no trouble with the law or anything, he starts killing the parents of friends in need. Of course, he doesn't tell them what he's doing – it's his little secret, pure charity. He's an anonymous benefactor, if you like.'

Madame Beck lowered her head in despair.

'Why don't you carry on writing for children? Your kids' books are doing well …'

'This is a kids' book! He's a really nice guy! He loves his mother, loves his friends, his friends' parents, he loves everyone, but these are tough times for all of us, aren't they? He kills people's parents the way Eskimos leave their elders on a patch of ice because … it's natural, ecologically sound, a lot more humane and far more economical than endlessly prolonging their suffering in a dismal nursing home. Besides, he'll hardly be doing them harm; he'll do the job carefully, every crime professionally planned and tailored to the person like a Club Med holiday. Plus there's nothing to stop us giving him his comeuppance at the end. I could have him murdered by the twenty-something son he hasn't seen for years, who's got in with a bad crowd. Or have him fall prey to a random act of violence, a mugging on the metro gone wrong, something like that … What do you think?'

Two hours later, Madame Beck was reluctantly handing me a cheque, barely able to look at me.

With that meagre advance, I've been able to rent a cottage by the sea from a painter friend of mine, where I've spent the past two months yawning so hard I've almost dislocated my jaw.

'I wake up in the morning with my mouth wide open. My teeth are oily: I'd be better off brushing them before bed, but I can never bring myself to do it.' These words of Emmanuel Bove's, the opening line of his novel *My Friends*, sum up my state of mind exactly. I put aside my typewriter – already thick with dust – and tackle tasks more suited to my skills: washing up, a bit of housework, starting a shopping list, bread, ham, butter, eggs ... I don't mind chores; they stop me beating a permanent retreat to my bed. Plus, routines are a useful way of preparing for the hereafter. Then I head to the beach, whatever the weather.

Today, it's glorious, a picture-postcard sky, framed by the inevitable seagulls. The beach is very close to where I'm staying – a five-minute walk straight down Rue de la Mer. It's always a surprise to see that mass of green jelly at the end of the road and the no-entry sign sticking up like a big fat lollipop on the horizon. You find yourself leaning forward as you walk, head down against the wind that stands guard along the front. There's something minty about the cold. You can clearly see the chimneys of Le Havre and the tankers waiting their turn at Passage d'Entifer.

When you are mute, or almost mute, certain words explode inside your head like fireworks: ENTIFER. Or even: TOOTHBRUSH. I never speak to anyone, only the woman in the tobacconist's on Rue de la Mer.

'Good morning, Madame ... How are you today, Madame?'

Like the sea, she's up and down – she lives above her shop and is never seen anywhere else.

There are two people on the beach. As they approach the waves, they stop and ponder whether to turn left or right. In the end they part ways, one sticking out her chest and grabbing an armful of sunshine, the other spinning on the spot, flapping the wings of her coat. She stumbles into the foam and re-emerges, knees held high. I can put up with happy people, from a distance.

I never walk far along the beach.

Yes, when I was first here, I went exploring, clambering over rocks and craggy outcrops, coming back exhausted, my pockets filled with pebbles, shells, bits of wood. Now I prefer to sit on the bench for old people. There are none of them here at this time of year – it's too cold. For a brief moment, I enjoy the exhilarating feeling of being right where I should be, a feeling made all the sweeter by my knowing exactly where I'm headed: back to humanity with a thud.

Here comes the 'thug'! I know him by his lumbering gait; he walks as if pushing an invisible wheelbarrow. Shaved head, face like a suitcase that's been dragged around the world, hands like feet and feet that make furrows in the ground, whether sand, concrete or tarmac. The man has a permanent black eye or a hand in plaster – they say he's always getting into fights. And yet everyone accepts him, puts up with him. I, on the other hand, am terrified of him. If it was up to me, he'd have been locked up long ago, or simply eliminated. He forces me to get up and walk further. But further is too far for me. I decide to head back along the beach.

I love trampling on shells; I imagine they're my editor's glasses. There's no one left now that the two people have gone, and the thug with them. I suddenly feel so alone it's as if I'm invisible. The sky shrinks back above my head like burnt skin. The silence bores into my ears. I'd give anything to be anywhere but here.

As for the others (the ones who weren't dead, not yet) they were like him, living flat on their stomachs in hastily built trenches, keeping watch for the snipers that were decimating their ranks. Reaching their forties was starting to feel like the path to the emergency exit.

Louis would happily spend the day in the children's room, crammed into the little bed like a vegetable in a crate. When he was little, he used to spend hours like that, in a state of boredom. No one should believe that good children sitting quietly are gentle dreamers, inhabiting marvellous worlds. No, they're just bored. Although the boredom of childhood is of a different quality, a sort of opium. Later on, it's hard to recall that feeling. Tedium has replaced boredom. The row with Alice yesterday evening, or rather its consequences, were part of the tedium.

Suddenly the little room was suffocating; the pleasant gloom had become a black cocoon pressing in on him. Louis jumped out of bed, pulled back the curtains and opened the window. He was hit by the light and the hammering of the pneumatic drill. He closed his eyes, grimacing, and staggered back to the little bed. There was a note stuck under the bedside lamp. Alice's writing.

'If you could be gone by the time I get back, that would be good.'

Of course, he had been expecting this for a long time, but why now? That stupid argument must have been the last straw. As if he cared what happened to him after his death! Now he was going to have to move out.

The impact of the sparrow against the glass of the half-open window made no more noise than a rubber ball bouncing on a carpet. Yet this little collision radiated like an electric charge through Louis from his chest to his groin. All his childhood fears were contained in that little ball of grey feathers, tiny bones, and quivering flesh now trapped inside the room by the curtain. Outside, the insistent thrumming of the drill was the counterpoint to the noise of the bird's panicked beak against the window.

'Go away!'

The bird froze in front of the window framed by the white sky like a bad painting. Louis closed his eyes, hoping the sparrow would escape by itself, but the tapping of the beak started up again, shattering the silence. All he needed to do was lift the curtain and open the window wide but Louis could not bear the idea of even the briefest physical contact with the idiot bird. He would need a long stick, a fishing rod, for example. What if the bird, in freeing itself, flew into his face? Birds always got in your face, like cats and spider webs.

A breath of air briefly lifted the white net curtain. Enough to allow the sparrow to propel itself through the beckoning gap. But it was a very young bird, to whom no one had ever explained the difference between inside and outside. And so instead of flying off it began to twirl about like a demented wind-up toy between the four walls of the little bedroom. Exhausted and terrorised, it came to rest wide-eyed on the corner of the wardrobe. The smell of fear turned the atmosphere of the room into a toxic, unbreathable acid. Then another draught arrived to waft the curtain. The bird spotted the white rectangle and recognised its territory, the great outdoors with no corners and no obstacles that stretched from never to nowhere. Ecstatic, it flung itself at the opening. It was halfway out when the window banged shut, cleaving it in two.

Open-mouthed, Louis watched as grey feathers floated to the carpet. Just then the phone rang.

'Hello? Yes, it's me. Good morning, Richard. No, I haven't forgotten I owe you money. Yes, I know, but ... everything's a bit tight at the moment ... Listen, Richard, I can't talk to you now, a bird has just been decapitated in front of me ... No, it's not another of my excuses! I swear, it's shaken me up. Why

don't we get together later, shall we say 12.30? ...
Where? Brasserie Printemps, under the dome ... And
why not? ... Yes, yes, I insist, it's a beautiful place.
Excellent, see you soon.'

Why did I call him Louis? After the old French coin,
because of his money worries? I must have been pissed
when I came up with that. I get silly when I've had a
drink, start playing around with words. Louis doesn't
suit him. He needs a younger, more contemporary
name. Like the guy at the other end of the bar, for
example – what's his name? ... I can hear it from the
mouth of the landlord serving him: Jean-Yves. I can't
imagine calling my hero Jean-Yves for 200 pages.

Though I can't claim to have done much to serve
the greater good today, I'm still feeling quite pleased
with my efforts. My word count is hardly spectacular,
but it's not a bad show for two hours' work. The bird
incident was what got me back in the swing of it. When
I opened my eyes this morning, I noticed that one of
the panes in my bedroom window was broken and a
fluffy white feather was caught in the Z-shaped crack.
I don't remember hearing anything, but I'm sleeping
deeply at the moment. Whatever it was, it could only
be a sign, an invitation to pick up my quill. I could have
written more but Hélène rang. Wants to take me on a
three-day trip to England. I'll be glad to see Hélène,

but why England? What's wrong with meeting up here?

After the phone call, I went back to the beach to watch the sun go down. The footprints in the sand are an odd reminder of all the people who've pounded up and down the beach, whom you'll never see. The sun was taking for ever to disappear, so I left before the show was over. On the way home, I stopped at a café for a half. I wasn't thirsty; I just needed some human company, to nestle among the other beasts in the stable. Plenty of people go out in their slippers here. The guy next to me's wearing a pair. He's a giant with tiny feet. Size 38 or 39, no bigger. I can't take my eyes off them. I've seen him around town several times but never noticed how small his feet were. I'd never caught the name of the café either, so I ask. They tell me it doesn't have one. Once upon a time the owner was called 'Bouin'. But it's changed hands several times since then. These days, you just go 'to the café' or 'to the tobacconist's', depending on what you need.

Staring into space as I wait for my pasta water to boil, I remember Hélène's phone call. Why on earth did I agree to this ridiculous trip?

'So, what d'you think? Good idea, isn't it?'

'Why don't we just chill out here for a couple of days instead?'

'No, thanks. I've seen enough of that place; it's a miserable hole.'

'But I've got work to do. I'm already pushed …'

'Exactly. What difference is a day or two going to make? If you're that worried, you could take the typewriter with you and work at the hotel. It's three days, not a voyage to the ends of the earth!'

'Three days in England isn't the same as three days here.'

'What are you on about?'

'I know what travelling's like! You cram so much into every day that it feels like two days in one.'

'For goodness' sake, you're such a homebody!'

'No, I'm not. I travel all the time, just not from place to place.'

'Don't you want to see me?'

'Of course I do. That's got nothing to do with it …'

After that, I continued to hear her voice but not the words. A bewitching melody was playing through the little holes in the phone in an unfamiliar and sweet-sounding language. I said yes. Then she hung up.

Now I'm really in the shit. She's coming to pick me up in two days' time. Two days is nothing – she may as well have said, 'I'll be there in two hours.' I'm looking at everything around me as if for the last time. I'll have to speak, and in English to boot! We'll get lost and have to ask for directions. I can ask for directions in English; I just won't understand the reply. That's not going to get me very far! We'll have to drive on the left, courting death at every crossroads. Hélène's obsession with avoiding all the places 'other people' go will mean she insists on experiencing the dingiest pubs, where I'll sit wincing while sailors drunk on beer make eyes at her. We'll have to lug heavy bags from one hotel to another in the pouring rain. I'll be among people in their natural habitat. Come to think of it, I'm in the same situation as Louis, forced to do things against my will because of the choice a woman has made. Suddenly I'm feeling a lot more warmly towards Louis. Telephone!

'Christophe, how are things?'

'Well, to be honest …'

'Is it Nane? What's happened?'

'No, she's fine – well, there's no change. It's not that, or not just that. I dunno. The kids, work, money, time passing, a bit of everything. I've been thinking of you by the sea, all that fresh air … If I could find the time, I'd really like to come and visit.'

'That would be great, only I'm going away the day after tomorrow.'

'Oh, really? Where?'

'To England, with Hélène.'

'Oh, nice! You'll have to tell me all about it. Right, I'll let you get on. I've got to dash over to Nane's place, doctor's coming round. Bon voyage, you jammy git!'

Hardly! True, next to his problems, mine seem on the mild side. His ex-wife Nane is dying in a studio flat somewhere in the sixteenth arrondissement of Paris.

Nane was as beautiful as a Sunday, as a day with no purpose, kind, intelligent, perfect. One morning, she walked out of the door without even saying goodbye, leaving Christophe to bring up two kids on his own. He never tried to understand, but carried on loving her as he always had done, like an ox faithfully pulling its plough. Fifteen years went by with no news of her, and then a year ago he bumped into her by chance. She's ill – very ill. He's been looking after her ever since, as Nane's mother ought to have done if only she wasn't a self-obsessed monster. All that woman has done for her daughter is allow her to rent one of the studios she owns in Paris – at an extortionate price – purely because it would have been a headache to have left her on the streets. If only Louis existed in real life. But he doesn't, and Nane is so exhausted that the inheritance would be no use to her anyway. Would he even get there in time?

I should have suggested Christophe and the kids come and spend a few days here. I thought about it, but I didn't do it. Faced with such an outpouring of sadness, I backed away. Hélène would call that selfishness. I disagree. I simply have a great deal of respect for other people's privacy, in good times and bad.

2

Just before jumping on the bus, Louis saw a well-known actor in the street, although he couldn't remember his name. He looked smaller than when he was on screen. Days when things like this happened weren't like other days. On the bus, he sat opposite a little old couple, both sleepy, one with their head on the other's shoulder. They were like two little old cigarette butts stubbed out on the seat. They gave off the smell of beef stew and waxed parquet. It was as if they were at home at siesta time. Louis was overwhelmed by a wave of emotion, which almost made him feel sick. It was more than tenderness; he was overcome with love for this adorable couple. It was ridiculous, for two stops he struggled to contain his sobs. Then the man gently shook the woman awake; his wedding ring caught the only ray of sunshine that day. A skinny little man took their place. He was carrying an enormous lampshade that he laid on his knees. Louis could only see his eyes and the top of his bald pate. He looked like a thing, an unusual, detachable object. When he left, two young people took his place. Louis hated them immediately. Especially the man. He looked as boring as all the hardware he had just bought at the DIY store, things for cutting, sanding, screwing, measuring, tightening and loosening. For each item he took out of the plastic bag, he read the instructions all the way through, in a low voice like a depressed vicar. The flat-chested blonde who was with him nodded as she listened, dull-eyed and slack-jawed. Their weekends must be a blast!

Under the plane trees, dead leaves glued to the pavement by the rain resembled pamphlets warning of the end of the world. Just before he reached Printemps, a knot in the crowd forced him to slow down. There was a figure, just visible between the legs of the passers-by. It was stretched out on the ground. One trouser leg was rucked up, revealing a pale, almost blue calf and a brown sock rolled down at the ankle of a shoeless foot. The shoe, an old one, was a little further along. A corpse! In newspaper photos of crimes or accidents, the victim had always lost a shoe. Instinctively, Louis looked up at the buildings on the street. The sniper had vanished.

As he pushed open the door of the department store, he was greeted by a gust of warm air and ladies' perfume which made his head spin. He was instantly horrified at the thought of any physical contact. Feeling bodies brush against his, he had the sensation he was paddling barefoot through slime, sinking into an obscene swarming mass, taking part in a disgusting orgy. He could imagine grubby underwear, soft white flesh, damp body hair, the sickening smell of sweat and saliva.

He felt a bit better when he reached the dome of Brasserie Printemps. The enormous umbrella of light caught the hubbub of conversation and the clinking of cutlery. He quickly spotted Richard, but didn't show himself. It was absolutely delicious to watch him playing nervously with his knife while looking at his watch or casting a mournful eye over the menu that was almost entirely composed of salads and desserts. He stood out amongst the prim and proper matrons and their granddaughters daubed with banana split.

I won't go and meet him. Anyway, I can't give him his money back. I have nothing to give him as security except a brilliant horoscope for the coming month. I'll leave him stewing there.

A kind of short sigh followed by a thud caused him to turn round. One of the grandmothers at a table near him had just collapsed, her head in her plate of crudités. There was grated carrot in her hair, and a round of cucumber clung to her right cheekbone. By her chair a newspaper with a screaming headline: AGEING SOON TO BE A THING OF THE PAST! No, there certainly wasn't any sign of the barrel of a rifle with telescopic sight under that shower of fragmented light filtering through the stained-glass panes of the glass roof. The shot could have come from any one of the facets of the giant kaleidoscope.

Louis ran out of the store and walked straight ahead for a long time. Then he sat on a bench, in a large park, the Tuileries, or maybe it was the Luxembourg Gardens. Out-of-work dads recognised each other from afar. There were dozens of them drifting along the avenues, one child clinging to their back like a wart, another dragging its feet in the dust while holding on to their father's hand. The dads greeted each other with a weary little conspiratorial smile: 'Welcome to the club.'

There was one beside Louis. He had his eye on a little girl who was sticking her fingers into a drain cover. They were still the fingers of a newborn, soft and pink like shelled prawns. She was burbling incomprehensible sounds full of wet syllables: *pleu, bleu, mleu*. Her brother, barely any older, was pedalling like a demon round and round the bench on a red tricycle. Other Michelin men, bundled up in their winter garments, threw handfuls of gravel, wooden lorries, spades and rakes at each other. Any object became a projectile in their hands. An hour spent in their company would drive you completely mad. Louis was not unhappy in his state of stupefaction; he was no longer aware of the cold or of the strident cries. Far in the distance gardeners made little piles of leaves, which they then gathered into one large heap. He would like that work, simple and monotonous.

The little girl nearby began to shriek. One of her fingers was caught in the grille. Things like that were always happening to children – life is full of holes and there are so many little fingers. The father got down on all fours, trying to moisten the child's finger with his spit, murmuring reassurance to her. The child was screaming so much she was turning blue. Women came over to proffer idiotic advice to the poor father, now red with shame.

'You should have used soap.'

'You think I come to the park with my pockets full of bars of soap?'

He was envisaging having to pull out the grille and carry it still attached to his daughter's arm, but the little finger finally came free with a popping sound. The gathering dispersed, disappointed. They had been hoping for the fire brigade. The father stuck a biscuit into his daughter's dribbling snotty mouth and hastily gathered up the strange assortment of items that children must always have with them – a disgustingly grimy fluffy rabbit, a broken toy car, a retractable transistor aerial, a single roller skate. Had he missed anything? Yes, the little brother, who was pedalling at top speed towards the open gates to the street where huge menacing buses passed, hungry for little boys on red tricycles.

'Quentin! Come back here immediately!'

We're all children of children. This unfathomable thought kept Louis going until nightfall, until the time when everyone goes home.

It's time to go to the beach, but I'm staying put. My throat's a bit sore and I've a slight temperature – excuse enough to slack off for the rest of the day. Goes without saying it's this England business that's knocked me for six. With a bit of effort, it seems to me I could be properly ill by the time Hélène arrives. I open the window, unbutton my shirt collar and fill my lungs with the icy air, heavy with moisture off the sea. There – now all I need to do is slip under the duvet fully dressed and spend the whole day sweating, while dulling my brain with German soap operas and game shows. All being well, I should hit between 38 and 39 by the end of the night.

Watching Inspector Derrick's adventures only serves to give me a stiff neck. I'm better off staring at the wallpaper. I lose myself for a good while in the intricate faded flower pattern on the walls, when suddenly I get the strongest sense that Nane has died, right this very moment – puff! – like a light bulb blowing. All at once, the babbling in my head fades, to be replaced by a surprisingly clear memory of Nane's last birthday. We were celebrating in the ridiculous studio her mother put her in, on the fourth floor of a modern building in the sixteenth arrondissement. The decor and furnishings are all her mother's doing. The place is dripping with gold fixtures and walls of sky blue and pink. Every room is fitted with carpet, right up to the loo seats. Nane has never been allowed to change a thing. But what does a bit of fussy decor matter to her when she's dying anyway? She's made do with pinning a few postcards above her bed and sticking some flowers in a vase – no more than you'd expect to see in a hospital room. She has set up home in her mother's place the way a hermit crab moves into another mollusc's shell. A bed with a TV facing it. She lives off her own death, self-sufficient. Just as Hélène feared, Nane had 'made herself pretty'. Lipstick and eyeliner only emphasised the sorry state of her poor face. There was Hélène, Christophe and me. We'd just had a glass of champagne. Nane was about to blow out the thirty-nine candles on her cake. It was too much for her; she couldn't breathe so we had to call an ambulance. Lying on the stretcher, her body under the blanket made no more of a mound than a closed umbrella.

I daren't call Christophe. I don't trust this sixth sense of mine. What if it's just my imagination trying to find an excuse not to go to England? Nane dying would blow the whole idea out of the water. It's possible to pray for things unconsciously and I wouldn't put it past myself to do so.

I'm eating leftovers of leftovers and half listening to the news on the radio when I hear a knock at the door. My first instinct is to find a weapon, but then I get a grip: it's only ten past seven — no one's killed at this time of night.

'Evening. I live next door. I'm sorry to—'

'Yes, I recognise you.'

'We don't like to intrude.'

'What can I do for you?'

'Well, see, the thing is ... our daughter's going to be on telly this evening. *Going for Gold* — you know, the game show ...'

'Yes.'

'Our TV's just stopped working, so we thought to ourselves, maybe the chap next door might ... if we're not disturbing you ... assuming you have a TV, that is?'

'Yes. I understand. Please, come in.'

'Oh, that's kind of you, ever so kind! ... Arlette, come on, he says it's OK.'

Monsieur and Madame Vidal have invaded my solitude. We sit smiling idiotically at one another. They look like a pair of shiny new garden gnomes.

'The TV's upstairs. You'll have to excuse the mess.'

'Oh, don't mention it. It's us who should be

apologising, barging in on you while you're having your supper.'

'No, no, I'd finished. Come on up – it's the first room on the left.'

I give the duvet a few whacks and sit my visitors on the edge of the single bed, twenty centimetres from the TV screen; the only way I can watch TV is sprawled on a bed. I feel as if I'm looking after two nicely behaved children.

'Ooh, it's starting!'

Since there's no room to sit next to them, I slide in behind them. Between Monsieur Vidal's shiny pate and the silver-blue lichen sprouting from his wife's head, the TV presenter's unappealing face appears, swiftly followed by those of the contestants wearing nervous or slightly crazed expressions. Among them is Nadine, twenty-seven, a teacher from Rouen, who takes the opportunity to say hello to her students as well as her parents, who have no doubt tuned in to watch her.

'There she is! That's our daughter. Gosh, doesn't she look awful!'

'Must be the nerves! You know how shy she is …'

Arlette's hand nestles inside her husband's. I have the curious feeling I must be at their house. I daren't move, in case they notice me there. I wonder who Nadine takes after most, her father or mother? Nobody or everybody? In fact she most resembles the TV presenter, bloated as if by a phantom pregnancy, with a look on her face that says, 'I may be ugly, but I'm highly intelligent.' We'd hate one another at first sight if we were introduced. She looks a nasty piece of work. How could such a lovely pair of people produce someone with such an inflated ego? And lovely people they are, I'd bet my life on it. This is the first time I've seen them up close, but I've often spotted them coming back from the market or from a walk, arm in arm, never in a hurry, protected, as though living inside a bubble. I've so often imagined and envied the admirably empty, clean and tidy little life they lead together, just the two of them. Every time I have a row with Hélène, and we each go home to our separate houses for the sake of preserving our precious independence, I think of them. Tonight they're in my home, watching my TV; I could touch them; they belong to me and not to the stuck-up little madam on the TV screen. I want them to adopt me, right now this instant! I'd be a very good son to them, and what's more, I live just next door. I could ask them to talk to Hélène, to stop the trip from going ahead …

'… contains theobromine. Once the seed has been roasted and ground, it is used to make a drink …'

'Cocoa!'

Father and daughter say the magic word in unison, a split second before the time is up.

'Cocoa! That's the right answer! And that makes you today's CHAMPION!'

For a moment the bedroom flutters with the sound of beating wings as my two angels spring to their feet, clapping their hands. Part of me begrudges that stiff little princess her victory, but it has clearly made the two old things very happy.

'It's not just because she's our daughter – you have to admit she was the best. Ever since she was little she's always been able to learn whatever she wanted, and she retains it all, doesn't she, Arlette?'

'Oh, yes! She's always been very hard-working as well. It's not enough to be clever, you have to put the time in too! Besides, they don't give a teaching degree to just anyone, do they?'

'No, of course not! Right, I think this calls for a drink. You'll have a glass of something, won't you? Ah, go on!'

They won't stop droning on about their daughter – what about me, huh? We head downstairs. I run three glasses under the tap and open a bottle of Chablis.

'You've got a lovely place here. All these pretty things and pictures; it's very arty. What do you do for a living?'

'It's not my house. I'm renting it from a friend of mine who's a painter. I write books.'

'Oh right …!'

I wait for the 'Oh right!' to come back down to earth, having been blown out into the stratosphere to make way for a toast to Nadine's starry future.

'To Nadine! Yum ... Nice wine, isn't it, Arlette?'

'Very nice! Well, we had you down as being in the film business. We thought we'd seen famous people coming in here. We just happened to notice, you understand! We haven't been spying on you.'

'Of course not. It's true, several of my friends are actors.'

'Aha! See, Louis? I was right!'

'Sorry, your name's Louis?'

'That's right. Why?'

'No reason. It's a nice name.'

'Oh, I dunno. Have to be called something, after all. And your name is?'

'Pierre.'

'Pierre's nice too. If we'd had a son, we'd have called him Pierre, wouldn't we, Arlette?'

'Yes, Pierre or Bruno. But we had Nadine.'

I offer them another drink. Louis accepts; Arlette covers her glass with her hand. Louis talks about the job he did before he retired, working on the railways. I hear him, but I'm not listening. I'm trying to find my features in his face and, of course, I succeed. The resemblance is actually quite striking. I wonder how Arlette has failed to notice.

'Anyway, enough about me, we've kept you long enough already ...'

'Yes, my husband does like to talk! ... Why don't you come for lunch with us tomorrow? It's market day. Do you like fish?'

'The thing is ... yes, OK, I'd love to.'

'We'll see you tomorrow then, Pierre! Thanks again!'

Why did I lie about my name? His really is Louis though ...

3

Louis's mother took all her medication for the week in one go on Monday morning so that she could be sure she wouldn't forget. That was her best day of the week. She laughed at anything and nothing, spent an hour staring at the pattern on her waxed tablecloth, moved her knick-knacks about and invariably ended up embarking on a complicated recipe for which she only possessed a fraction of the ingredients. At eight o'clock, she collapsed in a heap for at least twelve hours.

Louis could smell it from the end of the corridor, something overpowering that caramelised his nostrils and covered his face like a leather mask. The radio and the TV were both blaring. His mother, curled up on the sofa, reminded him of a box of spilt matches. She had the bones of a bird that jutted out at all angles from under her black dress. A tuft of mauve hair indicated her head. Louis turned the volume of the television down, switched off the radio and went into the kitchen, holding his breath, his hand held out towards the cooker knob. Two fossilised pork chops lay on the bottom of a pan coated with burnt chocolate. On the side a cookery book was open at page 104, 'Cocoa chicken'. Louis opened the fridge and unearthed a slice of ham, a yoghurt and an apple and returned to the sitting room. Before eating, he propped his mother up with cushions, arranged a pillow under her head and laid a rug over her legs. He really liked watching television with her, especially when she was asleep. It was a programme made by Mr Average for Mr Average about Mr Average. Louis didn't bother to try another channel. He watched the television, not what was on. Exactly like in the street, or anywhere. What was happening in front of his eyes was only a pretext to let his imagination wander. It could be anything or anyone.

Sometimes he would follow someone in the street until he got fed up. The last time had been at Gare de Lyon, a woman with a parcel. She had led him as far as Melun. It must have been about one o'clock and the train was half full. Louis had sat a few seats away from the woman so that he could watch her without her noticing. About fifty, a bony head and torso, but plumper from the waist down. She was reading a magazine, *Modern Woman*, her elbows resting on the parcel on her lap. The parcel was so well wrapped that it looked fake: brown paper perfectly folded, string taut and knotted into an elegant but solid bow, the name of the recipient written in beautiful block capitals (M— something or other).

The buildings got smaller the further they went from Paris: tower blocks, then four-storey buildings, single houses and finally a cemetery, just before the beetroot fields. Very soon, the same sequence repeated itself but in the opposite direction as they approached Melun.

Melun prison! The package! The woman was going to visit someone in jail. A son? Or a husband more likely. She wasn't the kind of woman to have children. Melun was for long sentences. How many years had she been making this journey? How many times a week? There was something at once sad and comic in this image of the frumpy woman with the words 'modern woman' in her hands. What on earth could the bloke have done to end up in prison? Killed for money? To give it to this woman? At Melun, Louis had let the 'modern woman' disappear into the crowd. He understood at once that Melun was a dismal town, flat and useless. He had drunk coffee as he waited for the next train back to Paris.

Louis's mother let out a little fart, very short, but loud. How much was she going to give him? A thousand francs, two thousand francs? She never refused to give him money, but she gave it sparingly, at little old lady pace, so that he didn't stray. Even when his father had been alive it had been like that. Benefiting from the invariable paternal siesta, she would take him aside in the dining room. Eight uncomfortable, immovable chairs stood round a table as solid as a catafalque. There was an enormous sideboard in which piles of plates slept peacefully except for the once or twice a year they were taken out. They practically never went into that room, except to polish the furniture, a ritual like going to put flowers on Grandmother's grave on All Saints' Day. The rare dinners they gave were always depressing affairs, with his father's colleagues or family members, a universe of adults as icy as the polished mahogany of the furniture. You had to behave well, which meant you couldn't do anything you wanted to do. The moment his parents opened the glass doors hung with lace curtains that separated the dining room from the sitting room, they were no longer the same people. They assumed a stiff bearing and spoke in low tones as if they were in a museum. They didn't like going into the dining room either; they much preferred the kitchen, but that was how it was – grown-ups had obligations, work and dining rooms. It was because of little things like that that Louis had refused to grow up, and at forty, he wasn't about to change his mind.

'Louis, are you listening to me?'

'Yes, Maman.'

'I already gave you a thousand francs for your car

insurance, and that was only two weeks ago. I'm going to give you another thousand but after that I can't give you any more. We have to have the garage door redone, you know, and that will cost an arm and a leg.'

'I told you, I'll pay you back!'

'Shh! Your father's next door. I would give it to you if I could, you know that; it's just ... at the moment ...'

Louis had not been ashamed of asking them for money. They had money, not much, but more than he had. His mother's face had been barely visible in the gloom. It was only when she had moved her head that there was a reflection off her glasses. They never put the light on until it was completely dark, either in winter or in summer. Not because they were miserly but out of respect for the memory of an era in which thrift was as much a virtue as a necessity. Louis's mother had opened the sideboard and removed some notes from an imitation-lizard-skin box. That was where she hid her meagre savings. Everyone had known it, but no one ever mentioned it. Like the dining room, his father's siesta or the tardy lighting up, it had been part of their little habits as tightly woven together as the twigs of a nest.

'Put that in your pocket, and don't tell your father.'

'Of course I won't. Thank you, Maman.'

On the other side of the partition, Louis's father had known perfectly well what was going on between mother and son and it was fine by him. It was part of their game. Louis had crammed the notes hastily into his pocket, which his mother disapproved of; you were supposed to fold notes neatly in two and keep them in your wallet.

'Right, Maman, I must run now – I'm going to be stuck in traffic. Say goodbye to Papa for me.'

At the end of the road, the entire house was framed in his rear-view mirror. If you had turned it upside down it would have begun snowing.

Something very strange was happening on television. His mother's date of birth had just appeared on the screen: 7/10/21. Louis turned the volume up.

'If anyone born on 7 October 1921 is watching, they should telephone us because they have just won this superb caravan!'

A sort of square igloo shiny with chrome filled the screen: WC, shower, folding double bed, electric hob, oven, fridge …

Louis's eyes widened, like a child in front of a big Christmas toy. He wanted that caravan, he wanted it all for himself. That was where he wanted to live and nowhere else. A brand-new life in a brand-new caravan. It was obvious to him that destiny had made this programme just for him. And that wasn't all. He wanted everything else as well, everything his mother owned, her meagre savings, the house, her life.

The roll of cling film lying on the table was not there by coincidence. There were no more coincidences, just the last pieces of a puzzle all fitting together perfectly. That was why his mother was turning over, offering her face to the film of plastic Louis was preparing to press over it.

'Now you are brand new as well, shining and without a wrinkle. This is not going to hurt you any more than the day you gave birth to me. You're giving me life for a second time.'

There was barely a sound, a soft breeze rustling leaves and fingers opening and closing. The old woman, packaged like a supermarket chicken, had just died without making a fuss.

For a second Louis remembered the lady with the parcel on the train, and her husband in jail in Melun. But that wasn't going to happen to him; this was just a family affair, just something between him and his mother. It was nothing to do with anyone else. A little sooner, a little later ... for his mother it changed nothing and for him it changed everything. A new life was beginning, a proper life, the life of an orphan.

4

To tell the truth, I don't care that the Vidals are stupid, boring and not especially nice. At the beginning of lunch it bothered me a bit, then I got my head down and focused on the grub and the plonk. I stuffed myself like a goose for foie gras, until they once again seemed beautiful, radiant, unique, the perfect couple. I could tell that my ebullience was causing a few raised eyebrows, but, after all, arty types are always a bit zany. Still, they seemed pleased to see me go after the Calvados coffees.

I love napping on the beach, sheltered from the wind, leaning back against the jetty, my feet buried in the sand, hands in my jacket pockets, face to the sun. Slow explosions of red, green and yellow behind my closed eyelids. When I was little, I used to love pressing my eyes or staring at light bulbs to make fireworks go off inside my head. Arlette used the most marvellous expression when talking about a friend of theirs with a drink problem: 'His face has been completely defaced by alcohol.' She comes out with a lot of things like that. It must have been partially aimed at Louis, who was starting to go glassy-eyed after the aperitifs. She stopped him showing me the scar from his operation. 'Not while we're eating!'

Three horses gallop by in the distance, down at the water's edge. I hear their hooves on the hard sand, slightly out of sync. That's how I've been feeling since this morning – just marginally out of step, slightly missing something. It's not an unpleasant feeling – halfway between spectator and tourist.

This morning, Louis – my Louis – killed his mother. So that's one thing ticked off. I've deflowered him. No sooner had I turned off the typewriter than Hélène rang; the England trip is on hold. (What a shame!) Problems at the newspaper, problems with her daughter, problems as far as the eye can see.

'Sorry, darling. Poor you. Is there anything I can do to help?'

'No, love. It's as if everyone made a pact to be a total pain yesterday. Nat went off on one! I don't know what's up with her at the moment.'

'She's sixteen.'

'Yeah, well, it's no fun. She's buggered off God knows where. If you hear anything from her, will you—'

'Of course, if she rings I'll let you know straight away.'

Poor Hélène, at the mercy of 'other people'. If only you'd listen to me ... We could shut ourselves up here for ever. We'd never go to England, we'd never go further than the beach and we'd see nobody, except the Vidals from time to time. They're really nice, you know; you don't have to try to be clever around them. We'd eat, we'd make love, we'd sleep fused together like Siamese twins. War and peace, summer and winter would come and go around us and we wouldn't notice. It would all be the same to us. What the hell do 'other people' have to do with anything? Remember the time we stayed in bed for forty-eight hours? Wasn't it wonderful?

'But we can't spend our whole lives in bed! What would we live off?'

We'd take a leaf out of my Louis's book, wouldn't we? Remember after the famous birthday party at Nane's, after we'd taken Christophe home? In the car, you said, 'What I find really upsetting is that she'll never get the chance to enjoy a share of her bitch mother's money. She could at least have travelled in the last year, done the things she's always wanted to do …'

'It's been years since Nane wanted to do anything. It's like she's living the same day over and over again.'

'Maybe, but it still leaves a bitter taste. When I look at all these old codgers who have more time and money than they know what to do with … My father gets a new car every two years – he only uses it once a month. My mother's always on the lookout for a new coffee machine – she's already got seven. Can you imagine? Seven!'

'You'll inherit.'

'Yeah, right! They're rock solid. Not that I'm wishing them dead, but—'

'But it's like our pensions – we'll be half dead ourselves by the time we get them.'

'Exactly. What about you? Don't you think you'd make better use of your mother's money than she does?'

'No question.'

'So it's only when you no longer want anything that you get to do whatever you like? It's a joke!'

'I can never retire anyway – I'll just have to live off my fame and fortune. As for you, if you're relying on Nat and her friends to pay for you, things are not looking good. Our best hope is for an epidemic to wipe out the old people this winter.'

'They've all been vaccinated.'

We sat in silence after that, torn between feelings of guilt for having parricidal thoughts and dreams of inheritance. It was a struggle to get out of the car; the night sky looked like a huge empty black hole, or a box of ether-soaked cotton wool for killing kittens. The next day was when we stayed in bed for two days.

I've run out of cigarettes. It's starting to get chilly; the wind has changed. I've kept my evening plans to a minimum: a yoghurt and then bed. All of a sudden I feel exhausted, tiredness weighing on me like a great damp coat. Quick pit stop at the nameless café, where I hear it's going to rain tomorrow. I count my steps as I walk back to the house. I stop at 341; there's someone crouching outside my door.

'Nathalie? … What on earth are you doing here?'

'Just popped over to say hi. Is it a bad time?'

'Of course not. Come in.'

A gust of icy wind seizes the chance to come inside the house with us. I have a devil of a time trying to shut the door.

'Louis! Haven't seen you for ages! You haven't really changed. A bit fatter maybe.'

'A little, yes. Hello, Solange, you're looking good.'

'If you say it fast enough! But there you go, you can't make something new from old bones.'

Louis thought otherwise. He smiled at the mother of his first wife, Agnès. A voice from inside the house put an end to this embarrassing exchange.

'Bring him in, Solange! You can't just stand there in the doorway!'

'Yes, of course. Come in, Louis! Oh! Gladioli – you shouldn't have! Thank you, Louis.'

Nothing had changed, although now the furniture, the walls and Agnès's parents themselves were coated in a fine film of dust. It had been years since he'd set foot in this house, ten years, maybe more. Raymond, probably reluctantly, turned off the television and poured glasses of Ricard. Solange was twirling about with the gladioli, arranging them in a shaped crystal vase brought back from a trip to Hungary.

'Cheers, Louis!'

'To your good health.'

'Raymond! These drinks are really strong!'

'So what? That's exactly what a reunion like this calls for.'

'Condolences for your mother, Louis – Agnès told us. How old was she?'

'Sixty-six or sixty-seven, I'm not quite sure.'

'Oh!'

Louis saw they were subtracting their age from his mother's and noting with horror the tiny difference. Then ...

'You know, we were really surprised to get your call the other evening, after such a long time.'

'I'm sure you were. It just occurred to me, after speaking to Agnès. Time passes so quickly.'

'It does, but nothing much happens in all that time, at least not to us. Just our daily routine. Can I get you another? Come on, just one more.'

That had been last week. From the window of his caravan, Louis watched the barges sliding along the Seine. He had parked his caravan in the Bois de Boulogne campsite. It was very quiet at this time of year. He had been here for two months, since just after his mother's funeral. He hadn't worried about her death for a moment. Everyone knew the state of her heart and how she took her medication all in one go. He was feeling good, as he had felt every day of the past two months. He wanted to communicate his happiness to other people. To let them know happiness was possible and it was important to believe in it. So he had opened his address book at 'A' and picked up the telephone. The first two 'A's had been out, but Agnès answered.

At first everything had gone well for Agnès but as time passed nothing was right any more. Jacques, the man she had been living with for seven years, had just lost his job, and hers wasn't going well either. Fred, the son she'd had with Louis twenty-two years ago, was nothing but a worry. She didn't know where he was, Holland, or England, but he was certainly caught up in some scam involving drugs. Hardly surprising, since Louis had never bothered doing anything for him. Well, anyway. The other two children though, the boy and girl she'd had with Jacques (and whose names Louis could never remember) were turning out fine. If only they had a bit of money, they would buy a van and go and sell *frites* and waffles far away from Paris, in those places where people are always on holiday; it would be a great life, but ...

Louis had listened all the way through to this

stallholder's dream and then had ended the conversation, promising to send Agnès a cheque. He'd felt quite emotional after he'd hung up. He knew Jacques, a decent sort who loved Agnès as he himself would have liked to love her, but had never managed to. It pained him to hear that they had worries. The cheque he would send them would obviously not be enough to satisfy their desire for escape, but there was another way he could demonstrate his generosity. Just above Agnès's number was the number for her parents. There are phone numbers you keep without knowing why, and then one day, you do know.

Halfway through the butter-rich meal, Louis was already feeling very full. He had to make a superhuman effort to follow the meanderings of the conversation, particularly when Solange was speaking. Raymond mainly contented himself with filling the gaps in the conversation with shrugs and meaningful nods of the head. All the stories were about the misfortunes of people Louis didn't know, or barely knew, but whom death or illness briefly brought to life.

'Yes, you do! You must remember Jean, "le grand Jeannot" we always called him! He was at your wedding. He was the one who did an impression of a dwarf by putting his jacket on the wrong way round and his hands in his shoes … Well, anyway, he's dead.'

And so on and so forth, like the report of a naval battle: 'Le grand Jeannot, sunk!' Retirement had been fatal for them. They were slowly shrivelling like two cheese rinds under a glass cover, deaf to everything that happened outside their own four walls. They were adrift on their own ever-diminishing ice floe.

'Don't get me wrong, we like Jacques, but he's too nice – people are always taking advantage of him. We help them where we can, but we're not Rothschild's bank! A little more coffee?'

Louis hardly spoke. Sometimes he corrected a date, or a detail about a memory from the time he had been their son-in-law. Gradually the conversation began to dry up and he could feel their embarrassment. They had always found him intimidating. Even when he had been with Agnès they had been reserved around him. They were wondering what he was here for. Louis would have liked to stroke them like two puppies in a basket.

'Right, I'd better be going. I've already taken up enough of your time.'

'Not at all! Come back and see us again from time to time. We've really enjoyed it, haven't we, Raymond?'

Raymond acquiesced with a nod of the head, which he used to glance at his watch. It was all right, he wasn't going to miss the beginning of his television serial. As he took his leave on the porch, Louis checked that the spare key was still in its place in the pot of geraniums. That was where it had been when Agnès still lived with them. No, nothing had changed.

5

The clothes I've been wearing for more than ten days lie scattered around my feet like shed skin: shapeless tracksuit bottoms, trainers missing their laces, an old paint-spattered jumper. OK, I've got a bit of a belly, but I have nice legs and hands. Hmm. Ish. Besides, everyone looks a bit of a twat standing butt naked in front of the mirror. My God, it feels so good to lie down when you're tired, to piss when you need to, to eat when you're hungry and drink when you're thirsty. It's things like this which really sell life to you, whatever the price. It's strange to hear sounds being made around the house by someone other than me. I've put Nathalie on the sofa in the study and already I'm regretting it. She's bound to sleep in until midday and I'll get no work done tomorrow morning. When I stay over at Hélène's, I like hearing them nattering in the bathroom before bed. From the bed, I picture them in front of the mirror, making faces or twisting their hair, knife-sharp fingernails unleashed on the slightest pimple. The wall between us and the muffling effect of the various objects they hold between their teeth as they talk (grips, tweezers, hair bands) stop me overhearing their secrets, but I sometimes catch the odd word:

'Nicolas? I finished with him a month ago!'

'No, not that pot, it's mine! It's not good for your skin anyway.'

Meanwhile I lie there with my arms under my head, smiling up at the ceiling, happy as a bean sprouting between two layers of moist cotton wool.

At the dinner table earlier, Nat told me she would only be staying a day or two, just long enough to calm down a bit. Things are not going at all well with her mother.

'She's a pain in the arse at the moment. You can't say anything to her. I don't know what's up with her.'

'She's forty.'

'Yeah, well, it's no fun.'

I've heard that somewhere else. And it's not just her mother; it's school, exams, what's the point? Life's shit, may as well just get used to it. Then there's AIDS, and being bored of the company of people her own age, and old people too. Basically she's fed up, so she's come to see the sea.

I made her eggs with a few leftover lentils. She wiped the plate clean.

'Is there really nothing for dessert?'

'No. I've been working all day; I haven't had a

chance to go to the shops. Depression obviously hasn't taken away your appetite.'

'No, it's the opposite. I eat ten times more.'

She's smoked all my fags, drunk I don't know how many coffees and never stops talking, sentence after sentence, cigarette after cigarette, throwing in literary quotations she may or may not have understood, all of them heavy with yearning for death above all else.

'Nathalie, look at yourself. You're like a Sicilian widow, all in black. How do you think—'

'It's the fashion.'

'I thought you didn't want to be like everyone else?'

'I wasn't talking about clothes.'

She still has an adolescent's fat nose which she hides by brushing her hair over her face. She still smells of sour milk. It's weird to see her here without her mother.

'Right, sweetie pie. I'm wiped out. You can sleep on the sofa in the study tonight. I'll sort you out a bed tomorrow. I can't face getting all the sheets and blankets out now. Is that all right?'

Yeah, yeah, whatever. She wasn't tired anyway; she was going to read.

'Oh, by the way, did Maman call?'

'Yes.'

'If she rings again, don't tell her I'm here.'

'You're asking a bit too much, now! You know perfectly well she'll be worrying.'

'Well, don't call her tonight anyway.'

'Fine. You can call her tomorrow.'

'We'll see. Don't you find her a pain in the arse sometimes?'

'No more than anybody else. Don't you think you can be a pain too?'

'That's different. She's the adult, it's up to her to be understanding.'

'Let's talk about it tomorrow.'

Tomorrow is such a handy thing. Everything you haven't done, everything you plan to do, tomorrow! That must be the most disconcerting thing about death – no more tomorrows. Other than when she gets it into her head to take me to England, Hélène is not too much of a pain in the arse. Apart from when we go to the supermarket: she's always realising she's forgotten something when we're already at the checkout. She'll leave me there on my own with a trolleyful of stuff, a queue of people fuming behind me and the cashier losing patience. When she eventually returns with that pack of cotton buds she absolutely couldn't do without, she'll take all the time in the world meticulously organising our purchases in bags before poring over the receipt line by line, and heaven forbid there's a mistake! She's a pain in the arse then, that's for sure. And when she decides she wants to have sex outdoors. I hate it: the pebbles, the insects, the sand and especially the excruciating feeling you might be being watched. There's nowhere more overpopulated than a quiet little spot.

Those are the only things we argue about. And they're probably what I'd miss most if we broke up. Earlier, Nathalie asked why we don't live together. I gave her the same answer she gave me about the clothes: 'It's the fashion.' It was supposed to be a clever quip, but the more I think about it, the more it seems to me that there's no other reason.

What's she doing? She's put some music on! An incessant beat is making the flowery wallpaper quiver. You can only hear the bass, like the blood pulsing inside a rotten tooth. I could bang on the wall, but I can't help immediately picturing myself in a long nightshirt, holding a broom in my hand. I could get up and tell her to turn it down a bit. I could, but I won't. I don't want to see her on the sofa, cheek in hand, a book open in front of her, bare arm hugging the curve of her hip, looking at me as if she's the one standing and I'm lying down.

6

I slept really badly. Was it the meal at the Vidals'? Nathalie's arrival? One guest and suddenly the house is overrun. I'm struggling to put my thoughts in order. I need to move; I can't decide if I'm coming or going. As predicted, it's 10.30 and there are no signs of life from Nathalie. I've missed my date with Louis and I'm pissed off. Her mother may be a pain in the arse, but at least she gets up at a reasonable hour. What now?

'Good morning, Madame Vidal.'

'Call me Arlette! I've made too much beef bourguignon and I wondered if ... Oh, sorry, I didn't realise you had company.'

Nathalie appears doing her best baby doll impression, wearing a long T-shirt, yawning and stretching, her hair all over the place.

'Morning!'

Arlette seems disappointed. She looks as though she might take the Tupperware back off me, but it's too late.

'If I'd known, I'd have given you enough for two.'

'I'm sure there'll be plenty, Madame Arlette. This is Nathalie, my girlfriend's daughter …'

'Oh, lovely, hello, Mademoiselle. Right, I must dash. See you soon.'

You hear, Loulou? His girlfriend's daughter! Arty people aren't just a bit zany, they've no morals either! That's what Madame Vidal will be telling her husband.

Nathalie scratches her bum and screws her nose up at the brownish-yellow substance inside the box.

'What's in there?'

'Beef bourguignon.'

'Yuck!'

'It's not for breakfast. I've bought you some jam and fresh bread.'

'You've been shopping already?'

'It's almost eleven. Right, I'd better get to work. Will you be all right by yourself?'

'Yep. Look at you all smart today. You've shaved and everything.'

'I got changed, so what? See you later.'

'I don't understand, they were always so careful, especially with the gas.'

Agnès's hand trembled as she raised her glass of kir. Mourning really didn't suit her. Death is always a bit contagious. Louis hadn't expected her to be dancing a polka, but all the same, he felt she was taking it too far. 'You know, when you get older, you sometimes forget. What's so stupid is that it was caused by the bell ringing.'

'I'm sorry?'

'The postman ringing the bell, the explosion. It's a shame about the house.'

'Oh yes, the house. Yes, but we're still going to sell it, somehow or other. I just can't take it in. I'm an orphan.'

'So am I! It comes to everyone sooner or later.'

'Yes, but both at the same time!'

'Perhaps it's better like that. They were together until the very end. Imagine your mother all on her own ... or even worse, your father ...'

'Yes, OK, but they were in good health, happy ...'

'For how long? Think about Jacques, your children, you. You're going to be able to buy your van selling *frites*; you're going to be able to escape, live how you want. I'm sure that would make them happy. In a way, it's their last gift to you.'

'Of course, of course. And you, how is it in your caravan?'

'Yes, very good. It feels like living on a boat that doesn't go anywhere. It's fun. How is Fred?'

'I hardly saw him at the funeral. He looked like an unmade bed. I'm afraid that no one can do anything for him any more. Do you think about it sometimes?'

'Yes, obviously. I've never known how to act

with children – I'm a bit too like a child myself; I understand them too well to be a good father and I'm too old to be their friend. He's right not to love me, it's understandable.'

'Doesn't it bother you?'

'Yes, it does, but I'm sure we'll see each other one day, and that will be the day I'll be able to help him, to redeem myself in a way. I've always thought that.'

'You're very easy on yourself, as usual. What if he dies before you? It's perfectly possible, you know.'

'Then I won't get away with it.'

Louis was bored with the conversation. He was disappointed. Disappointed that he had failed in his work (although how could he have predicted that the postman's ring would make part of the house explode? The carbon monoxide from the boiler whose flame he had blown out at night should have been enough), disappointed also by Agnès's reaction which he had hoped would be more ... well, positive. But in any case, time was a healer, and in the end she and Jacques would accept their happiness. It was a first attempt, so certain little errors were inevitable. And some things are unforeseeable. But it was a shame – Raymond and Solange had been sleeping like babies when he'd left them. They must already have been dead when the explosion happened. Apart from the shock, the postman had only suffered some little scratches on his face. The next time, Louis would try to avoid this kind of hitch. At the next table, a couple their age were talking about a Monsieur Milien. They kept repeating the name.

'I said to him: Monsieur Milien, you may be the head of department but that does not give you the right to tell me how to bring up my son. He had nothing to say to that!'

'Milien is a jerk. So did he give you your money?'

'Yes, but he didn't really have a choice.'

Louis would have liked to see this Monsieur Milien. Just see him, that's all.

'Agnès, I've got to go, I have a meeting. I've enjoyed this. Stay strong. You'll see, everything will work out. Kiss Jacques and the kids for me.'

As he left her in the bleak café, Louis felt like someone who's abandoned his dog on the motorway. It's not easy to learn to give without receiving. April is a tiring month. You never know how to dress – coat or light jacket? – you're too hot, too cold ... but it's pretty. Louis felt he was growing a halo.

7

I won't trust modern technology until it's 100 per cent reliable, which is yet to be the case. My typewriter has packed up – it's gone mad, thrown the tabulation all over the place, messed up the line spacing, basically added to the general disarray. I have to try to remind myself that machines are supposed to be at the service of men, though cracking the whip isn't likely to fix a typewriter. I don't get on well with machines, I don't know why – it's a curse. There's not a coffee machine that doesn't spurt in my face, a car that doesn't belch at my approach, a remote control that doesn't leap out of my hands to remind me of my age, the Stone Age. In the old days, the worst that could happen was your ink pot might tip over. Now, on a Monday at the beach in Normandy, where am I supposed to find someone to repair a typewriter?

'It's ready.'

What's ready? ... Oh, yes, I'd forgotten, there's someone in my house. What a weird smell! ... Nathalie's dream of no longer being Nathalie suits her.

'I've made you a Chinese thing. Rice with your neighbour's leftovers. What do you think?'

'It's … a bit strange, but it smells nice.'

'Is something wrong?'

'My typewriter's packed up … Jesus, it's hot!'

'I put some chilli in it. It's meant to give you a hard-on.'

'Why would you want to give me a hard-on?'

'I dunno, I thought that's what men needed.'

'Not all the time.'

'I've done a dessert. Crème fraîche with raspberry jam.'

I wolf down the spicy nursery food, every so often glancing at her over the bowl. The house isn't cold, but even so, walking around the house in a vest …

'Aren't you cold, dressed like that?'

'No. Do you think I should be putting my thermals on?'

When she smiles, all her teeth show, little porcelain miniatures that remind me of my grandmother's coffee set. I lower my eyes, and they settle on her breasts. The image of my grandmother's china vanishes, giving way to an uncertain no-man's-land I daren't venture into.

'Mmm. That was delicious! We could pop down to the beach if you feel like it.'

'Have you seen the weather? It's pissing down.'

'Quite right. I hadn't noticed.'

I can't think of much else to suggest besides the

beach. I persevere, because of that uncertain no-man's-land.

'With a good raincoat on ... It'll get the blood pumping.'

'Off you go then, but I'm going to stay here and watch TV. *Inspector Derrick* will be on in a minute. I love falling asleep in front of it.'

'I think I'll call a place in Trouville about hiring a typewriter.'

'OK. I'll bring you a coffee.'

I hit the jackpot with the first number I ring. They've more typewriters than they know what to do with. If I pop in around four o'clock, I can take my pick. This is disconcerting, not to say disappointing. I had allowed myself to think I might have to spend a few days doing enjoyably little. Never mind. We can still make the most of the next two hours with a pillow under our heads and the TV at our feet. Nathalie brings the coffee; all that's missing is a little white apron and a Portuguese accent.

'Careful, it's hot! ... Can I get under the duvet? I'm cold.'

'If you like, but why don't you just put a jumper on?'

'The duvet's better.'

She slid in like an eel, forcing me to the very edge of the bed.

'Why are you all the way over there? You'll fall out and break something.'

'No, no. I'm fine. Ah, here we go, it's starting.'

'Better off here than getting soaked on the beach, aren't we?'

'Yes, but shush or you'll have no idea what's going on.'

'Yeah, right! It's always the same on *Inspector Derrick*. The murderer's always the wife. She kills her husband because he's been cheating on her with a younger woman. Just wait – he'll explain it all at the end over a beer.'

'Why do you bother watching it then, if you know what's going to happen?'

'Children only ever like one story. You've been writing them long enough, you should know. Why don't you take your shoes off?'

'Because this way, if there's a fire, I'm ready to go. Now, are you going to let me watch it?'

'OK, OK! Grumpy old fart …'

Nathalie's asleep well before Derrick solves the crime. It was indeed the wife who did it. Nathalie's head weighs more heavily on my shoulder than I'd imagined. Her hair smells clean and new. I daren't move a muscle, for fear of waking her, waking myself. A delicious state of torpor. I remember those first dates at the cinema, the heat of the other person radiating in the darkness, your head spinning until you forgot where you were, the actors on screen doing exactly what you wished you were doing. Fingers edging closer together on the arm of the chair, millimetre by millimetre … Wait, what am I thinking? Slowly, slowly, I pull myself free, slide a pillow under her head where my shoulder had been, and tiptoe out of the room.

'Oh, Hélène's in a meeting, is she? … No, there's no message. I'll call back later. Thanks, bye.'

8

Richard always ate like a pig, but today he was really stuffing himself.

'I was amazed to get your call. I had stopped believing I would ever get a cheque from you. I was angry, you know, but more about you standing me up in that bloody Printemps dome than about the money. You kept me hanging about with all those old bags and their grated carrot and Vichy water! You bastard!'

'I'm sorry, it was the day my mother died.'

'Never mind. So just like that you're suddenly loaded?'

'Well, a bit more comfortable, yes.'

'So you've suddenly acquired some principles? You're paying your debts. You're weird. In your place, I'd have fucked off. Actually, you've always been a bit—'

'A bit what?'

'I don't know, a bit like a Martian. Don't you want your *museau vinaigrette*?'

'No, go for it.'

'Thanks, I love that stuff. Listen, your call was great timing. I don't care about your cheque. But instead, you could do me a huge favour. I've promised to take Micheline and the kids to Deauville next weekend. But ... but I've a new secretary, as appetising as a leg of lamb on a fresh tablecloth, if you get my meaning?'

Richard glanced at Louis, and his glance was not appetising; his eyes were yellowish and bloodshot.

'You want me to be your alibi?'

'You've got it! I can't use the work crisis excuse again, I've used it too often. Micheline's always had a soft spot for you. Losers, they always turn her on. Anyway, if you help me out, you won't just be freeing me up, you'll also make me look like a devoted old friend. I win on all counts. If you agree, I'll tear up your cheque, OK?'

'OK, but keep the cheque.'

Richard stopped chewing, his fork in the air.

'I don't get it; you're even more bizarre than I thought. OK, whatever you want. I don't care either way. So we're agreed?'

Louis had woken up with a vile taste in his mouth that morning, and memories of a dream about Agnès, rape, blood, things that stuck in his mind like a morsel of veal stuck in a hollow tooth. He felt sticky with grime that no soap could wash away. It was because of that nausea that he had phoned Richard. Ever since he was a young child, Richard had always been his yardstick for disgust, a reference. At twelve, Richard was already a great big lecherous fool of a degenerate, who always dragged him into his sordid affairs from which he emerged humiliated and ashamed but curiously purified. These descents into sordidness were like a sort of redemption for him. Louis had ordered the same food as Richard. To eat like him was to start eating him.

'You didn't reply.'

'Yes, yes, I'll do it.'

All through the *îles flottantes*, Richard reeled off salacious stories about his clients, his mistresses, his friends' wives. His world was one long gang bang, unending fornication. Louis wasn't listening, he was watching, fascinated, as Richard's lips twisted like two slugs as they greedily took in the food. There was something of the abyss about that mouth in action; it was like watching a mysterious black hole.

'What about your son — is he still injecting?'

'Yes, he still is, I think.'

'You're not saying much, don't you care?'

'There aren't many opportunities for young people at the moment.'

'Hmm … if one of my kids tried that, I'd put him back on track with a boot up the arse. But it's not my business. So, shall we go? Leave it, I'll pay.'

They were on the platform and just as the metro emerged from the tunnel, Louis thought of Richard's children. A shove with his shoulder and Richard was no more than a signature at the bottom of a will. Louis was already far away down the corridor leading to another line when the crowd reacted. He smiled as he reflected that his cheque for five thousand francs would go to the children of the great fat pig, even if they didn't need it.

9

Good riddance to that prick Richard. I can't stand people I'm indebted to, and I had the urge to hurt somebody. I dashed off those last few pages in a bad-tempered scrawl but I feel no better for it. I need to get out.

'Nathalie! Do you want to come with me to Trouville?'

'Can we eat out?'

'If you like, but we have to go now.'

Through the windscreen, the rain is turning the landscape into a child's daubed painting, all the colours mixed up to make a pooey grey-brown. The horizon has gone, the sky's dripping from top to bottom and the town is reduced to a puddle.

'Drop me off at Prisu. I feel like buying myself something from the supermarket, any old thing.'

'OK. Let's meet at Les Vapeurs.'

The guy has rented me a little Canon, guaranteed to make very little noise, and so responsive you need only blow on the keys to get them working. The exact opposite of what I like – I'm going to really miss the

Kalashnikov rat-a-tat of my old tank. I've been waiting at Les Vapeurs for half an hour. I'm not a fan of the place, but it's a bit like a Paris bistro, and since Nathalie doesn't like anywhere but Paris, she should approve. Here she is at last, beaming as if the tooth fairy's just been.

'What are you drinking? I'll have the same.'

The bitter taste of the Picon bière gets the thumbs down from Nathalie. She rummages inside a plastic bag and pulls out a little pair of lacy knickers which she holds over the lower half of her face like an exotic dancer.

'Cute, aren't they? I got the bra to match.'

'Put that away, Nathalie.'

'Why, are you embarrassed?'

'No. You're being silly, trying to get a reaction.'

'Fine! … Ugh. This Picon bière stuff really is foul.'

'You should have ordered a grenadine. Where do you want to eat?'

'Dunno, wherever's most expensive. That place we went with Maman — you know, the up-its-own-arse one.'

Toile de Jouy on the walls, crushed velvet seats, seafood platters and obsequious waiters to whom I find myself presenting Nathalie as my daughter. It's the first time this has happened and it feels slightly humiliating. Nat wants wine and so that's what we drink, and if she wanted to go and look around Honfleur, we'd do that too. The part of me that keeps the other part on a tight leash, the part that is aware of the appalling banality of the situation, gradually cuts it some slack, worn down by such stupidity. So, with my neck collared and eyes red, I trip over my lead, start talking about my book, how Louis eludes me, does things I wasn't expecting, kills people his own age …

'All this stuff about your book is going right over my head. If I ever get married, it'll be to someone with a proper job.'

'What's a proper job then?'

'I dunno … lumberjack, architect, plumber … Shall we get out of here?'

We head back to the car with a fishy aftertaste in our mouths and an incredible urge to giggle. The gingery moon looks like a cigarette burn in an orphan's cape. The scent of escape hangs in the evening air. An English couple ask us the way to Ouistreham. I don't think they understand my directions. By the time we get home, I've shaken off the leash completely. There's the dregs of a bottle of white wine and half a bottle of Negrita. I'm determined to keep going until the small hours, but I proceed timorously, using Louis as my shield.

'Do you have to keep going on about that loser? Why don't you put some music on instead?'

My collection consists of a few old scratched records, the sound scarred, as if the tracks had been recorded in front of a wood fire. I pick the top one off the pile and place it on the turntable. I watch it spin, arms lolling by my sides like a village idiot.

'Shall we dance?'

'I can't dance.'

'It's a slow number – it's designed for people who can't dance.'

I must look as stupid as a seagull prancing on sand. I say as much to Nathalie and she tells me to shut my gob. Without my gob, I'm nothing. I let myself go like a floppy puppet, feeling my ears turn as red as a tobacconist's sign. The armful of youth I am holding against my body is bringing a flood of long-forgotten memories to the surface. I enjoy the moment all the more for knowing I'll regret it bitterly tomorrow morning. A last-ditch burst of morality saves me just in the nick of time. I pull myself free, stagger over to the sink and run my head under the tap, which looms like the guillotine.

'Right, Nathalie. I think it would be better if I went to bed.'

'Better than what?'

'It would just be better. Look, I may be pissed but come on, the spice, the snuggles, the frilly underwear, the slow dances … Don't you think I can see it coming a mile off? If you've got a score to settle with your mother, just ring her.'

'Oh, calm down! Leave my mother out of it.'

'That's exactly what I'm trying to do.'

'Yeah, right! You're too scared to sleep with me, that's all.'

'Nat, you're really getting on my nerves. I'll do what I want, thank you very much. Besides, I've got a beer belly, I stink of Negrita, and … and afterwards? Have you even stopped to think about the consequences?'

'No, I'm sixteen. Anyway, for fuck's sake, it's not exactly complicated! What if I fancy guys with beer bellies who stink of Negrita? And what if—'

The telephone stops her short. It's Christophe telling me Nane has died.

10

A little white Scottie had just run under the bench where Alice and Louis were sitting. It was a bench the little dog knew well; it was just the right height for scratching its back. A little further away, on the road, a woman of a certain age in the beige mourning of the modern woman called the dog in a deep voice, 'Rimsky!' Behind her were two ponds, two twinkling mirrors, only slightly wrinkled by the skimming flight of the ducks. Alice and Louis watched the little dog as it bounded off to join its mistress. Neither of them said so, but they were both thinking that this was just like three years ago when they had just met each other. There had followed three or four months of a happiness as round and smooth as a boiled egg, like the two ponds they often visited, that gave them the vertiginous impression of eternity. It was the beginning of summer. Alice's children had been despatched to their grandparents. Louis had just spent an appalling winter living with his mother. Then the clouds had lifted. By a happy coincidence he had found himself acting as intermediary in a property transaction and had earned himself thirty thousand francs whilst barely lifting a finger. A very happy period, in which he had felt invincible.

'I still don't understand it! You disappear completely for six months. Then yesterday you call up as if nothing has happened!'

Louis tapped his shoes together to get the dust off. 'It was never the right moment.'

'The right moment? We'd lived together for three years! You just disappeared from one day to the next, as if you no longer existed, all your things still in the house, the children asking where you were … It was as if you were dead!'

'My mother died; I had a lot to organise … It wasn't the right time.'

'But now, it's the time to reappear? You come and go in people's lives as you please.'

'You told me to leave. Don't you remember your little note?'

'Oh, please, it's not as if it was the first time. We row, we separate for a couple of days so that we can cool off and then … Well, anyway, what are you going to do now?'

'I've written you a cheque.'

'I don't give a stuff about your cheque! It's us I'm talking about.'

'But you said you were in the shit at the moment.'

'I've been in the shit for years and years as you well know. I don't care!'

'You're wrong, it's important – you should care.'

'And that's coming from you? Have you fallen on your head, Louis, or is it the inheritance from your mother that's made you blow a fuse? The old bat is doing you as much harm dead as she did when she was alive.'

Louis got up from the bench and took a few steps towards the pond. There were ducks, moorhens, catfish, frogs and turtles. There didn't use to be when they came before. The turtles were new. They climbed on top of each other, like mussels, then kept still, their heads up to the sun.

'Are your parents in Kalymnos at the moment?'

Louis turned round but the reflection of the sun from the pool of mercury behind him prevented Alice from seeing his expression. Even when she put her hand up to shade her eyes, she could only see him as a dark shadow.

'Yes, like every year, why?'

'Oh, nothing. I was looking at the turtles; they reminded me of your parents.'

'Thanks very much! Don't stand on the edge of the water, it's blinding me. I can't see you – it's like speaking to a ghost.'

Louis came back and sat down beside her. He could have asked her for news of the children, or complimented her on her new haircut, or reminisced about the time they used to come here, but he didn't. All the sentences he prepared in his head seemed to him to ring hollow and died before they crossed his lips. It wasn't just an impression; she *was* talking to a ghost haunting a well-known landscape. He wasn't talking, he was reciting. A role learnt by heart, without conviction, and the more he became aware of this, the more he felt himself shrinking, fading, crumpling up like an old tissue. He didn't dare look at her for fear of seeing two large tears forming on her lashes. Her face would be scrunched up, her mouth drawn down and her lower lip would be trembling almost imperceptibly. She would look ugly and a bit ridiculous, like everyone does when they cry. And there wasn't anything else she could do other than cry.

A group of children charged down one of the paths, shrieking. It was like a bag of balls tipping over. Two teachers puffed after them like two seals. 'No, don't go so close to the edge!'

A dozen little round white tykes lined up in front of Alice and Louis. 'Look at all the tadpoles! And the swimming tortoise! M'sieur, come and see the tortoise swimming!'

The arrival of the children provided a distraction for Alice and Louis, allowing them to relax a little. Louis stood up, massaging his stiff neck. Alice sniffled, looking for a handkerchief in her bag. Her voice was croaky when she said, 'There are turtles in the pond?'

'Yup, loads of them.'

'There didn't use to be. Turtles live a long time, don't they?'

'Very.'

One of the children, flat on his stomach at the edge of the water, had just caught one. He got to his feet, brandishing it over his head, and ran off, chased by the other kids.

'I caught one! I caught one!'

One of the teachers set off in pursuit.

'Stéphane!!! Put that back in the water immediately!'

Just before the teacher reached him, the kid threw the turtle as hard as he could into the water, like a stone. For one moment there was a commotion in the reeds. The moorhens and ducks fled the turtle bomb in a flurry of wings. The teacher slapped Stéphane, the children dispersed and the water closed around the flying turtle. Very quickly, it was as if nothing had happened. There was dead calm.

'Water is crazy; you can't make holes in it. If you threw an atomic bomb in, quarter of an hour later, there would be nothing, barely a ripple.'

Louis wasn't certain he had spoken out loud. He said, articulating clearly, 'Strange day for that turtle.'

'Not only for that turtle.'

He had anticipated that response as if everything had been preordained, like a moment ago, before the arrival of the children. It was exasperating, that feeling of being nothing but an interpreter of a scene that was taking place elsewhere. Alice rose, putting her bag over her shoulder.

'Let's go, Louis. I want to go home. I expected something else. I find this painful.'

Louis wanted to reply 'Me too', but it wouldn't have been true. It was the absence of pain that worried him. From far off, they could have been mistaken for a couple of old people.

After leaving her at Gare Saint-Lazare with a weak smile, Louis went into the nearest travel agent. The girl who sold him the ticket for Greece had lank hair, circles under her eyes and bad skin, a skin that bruised easily – poor circulation. He would have liked to know her parents.

11

Sometimes I wish I was dead or, better still, that I had never existed. I had an awful night filled with corpses hanging above my head like hams. And then this morning I remembered I had to get the corrections for one of my kids' books in the post today. This one little chore suddenly seemed like the perfect opportunity to rejoin the land of the living. My salvation lay at the post office. I entered the building as if stepping inside a church (or more likely a mosque – I was losing my religion after all). There were three people ahead of me. An old man like origami, folded into eight, and two younger old women gossiping in low voices.

'… and that's exactly what I told her.'

'You didn't?'

'I did!'

'You mean you said—'

'What I just told you, right to her face!'

'Blimey, you're a one …'

What could the old tart have said, and to whom? Something nasty, no doubt. She had clearly been saying spiteful things all her life – they had twisted her mouth into a kind of harelip. There was plenty of other stuff in my upturned dustbin of a head that could have done with clearing up, but I simply had to have the answer.

'What did you say to her?'

The pair of grannies looked at me as if I had just spat in their faces.

'Are you having a laugh? … Mind your own business! Really. It's got nothing to do with you!'

'Yes, it has! I might know the person you've been saying horrible things about.'

'But … I didn't say anything horrible! What's the matter with you? You should see a doctor!'

'Fine, I'm not going to push it, but it wouldn't have cost you much to tell me, would it?'

'That's enough! Leave us alone!'

I shrugged. Let her keep her little secrets. Nothing else happened after that; the talk turned to purely postal matters. The two old ladies looked daggers at me as they left, screwing their fingers into their temples.

The post office having failed to deliver the serenity I'd been counting on, with my head spinning I try again by having a second breakfast and taking a second shower. I try to tell myself things are looking up. Nat's still asleep, or dozing, tangled up in the bedclothes. I'm glad; I don't know what I could think to say to her. I didn't know what to say to Christophe either when he told me Nane had died. I could have answered, 'You poor thing, I'm sorry; maybe it's for the best. Do you want me to come over? Do you want to come here? Is there anything I can do?' All I said was, 'Oh', followed by a silence that seemed to go on for ever. Christophe put an end to the exchange of sighs, saying he'd call me tomorrow; he needed to rest. I mumbled something incomprehensible and Christophe hung up. Nat raised an inquisitive eyebrow.

'Nane died.'

'Shit ... Do you want a coffee?'

She was filtering it when the phone rang again. It was Hélène.

'Nane died.'

'I know. Christophe just called.'

I couldn't take in what Hélène was saying. My brain had become so slow, it struggled to process every single word. Nat was sulking, having realised it was her mother on the other end of the line.

'Hello?'

'Yes, I'm here.'

'You weren't saying anything. I thought we'd been cut off.'

'No, I'm listening.'

'Is there someone with you?' (Silence.)

'No, why?'

'I don't know. I just got that impression.'

'No, it's the kettle; I put some water on to boil. Sorry, I'm just a bit stunned.'

'Me too, even though we were expecting it. OK, I'll let you get on. Shall I call tomorrow? Oh, by the way, you haven't heard anything from Nat, have you?'

'No, nothing.'

'That girl, she can be such a pain in the arse when she wants to be! Still, I'm not going to get the police on her back. Let me know if …'

'Promise. Speak tomorrow.'

I've lied a lot in my life, and come off none the worse for it, but this time I struggled to swallow my first mouthful of coffee. Nothing seemed to want to go in or out. Like a millstone around my neck, this enormous lie was going to drag me into the void, that is, into an endless succession of bigger and bigger lies, weighing on me more and more heavily.

Nat was perfect. I expected nothing, she gave nothing. After this second phone call, she threw her head back and blew out an invisible puff of smoke. 'Right, shall we go to bed then? That'll do for today.' She put the mugs in the sink and gave the table a wipe. If you didn't look too closely, you could mistake this for a normal house with normal people in it. 'You' could; I couldn't. There was nothing normal about the way her rump wiggled its way upstairs, or her presence in my bedroom or her body under the sheets; still less my body, which did not feel like my own, and struck me as fairly unappealing.

'You know, if you've changed your mind, it's OK.'

I turned to face her. I wished I could say a word to her, 'the' word, the one you'd take with you to a desert island, the word before words, that would say everything and nothing all at once. It was silenced before it was said, an oblong speech bubble on the edge of her lips. I had never tasted her lips, only her cheek. It was enough to make me go back for another helping. I thought of all those people in war-torn countries with nothing to do after the curfew but make love. No electricity, no TV, no heating, just fucking, with the glorious energy of despair. But I was at war with no one but myself. The best part of me, or the least worst, had refused to enter the bedroom and stood scowling in the doorway as the other part of me tired itself out with weary embraces.

'Forget it, you've had too much to drink.'

I didn't try to persuade her otherwise or apologise. I simply made a mental note of the fact it was two in the morning and I had at least a few hours of sleep ahead of me, during which the rest of the world could crumble for all I cared.

Sadly, the world did not crumble, and here it is again in the guise of Arlette Vidal, whose shadow I can see through the curtain. Knock, knock …

'Morning! Here, I've brought a pot of jam for our young friend – it's home-made! They love sweet stuff at her age.' (Circular glance over my shoulder in search of evidence of debauchery.) 'Listen, we've just had a new TV delivered, but Louis can't seem to tune the thing. He's not very technical, and on top of that he's a bit off colour this morning. I don't suppose you'd be able to pop round and have a look?'

It's that or stare into my breakfast bowl.

'I'll be round in two tics, Arlette.'

Louis does have an odd-looking complexion, a nasty pair of bags under his eyes and shortness of breath.

'Not feeling too great, are we, Monsieur Vidal?'

'Oh, it's nothing, bit of a chest infection. It's this sodding television that's really not right. We can't make head nor tail of it – it's all written in American.'

After a good fifteen minutes, I manage to get a steady picture and show the local news in glorious Technicolor. The Vidals are happy, channel-hopping like mad things with the remote control.

'We didn't have one with the old set. Now we'll never have to stand up!'

Louis's spluttering with joy – who cares about the chest infection, he doesn't have to stand up. If only I could spend the day here with them, sitting in front of the new TV and nibbling sponge fingers. The three notes of the doorbell chime along with the news theme tune. Arlette gets up and trots over to the door like a wind-up toy.

'It's your step-daughter … what's her name again?'

'Nathalie.'

She's waiting on the doorstep, dishevelled, red-eyed, wrapped up in my parka.

'Your friend Christophe has just arrived.'

'Christophe! Excuse me, Madame Vidal. See you later.'

'OK, see you later.'

Nat utters a vague 'M'dame' which goes rolling into the gutter between an apple core and a crumpled packet of Winstons.

'Man, it stinks of cabbage in there! Smells of old people.'

'Has Christophe been here long?'

'Half an hour. I was waiting for you to turn up – I didn't know where you were. He's got a weird look about him, your mate, as if the lights are on but no one's home.'

12

Alice's parents' boat was anchored some way out from the coast. It was a huge effort to reach it and he was completely exhausted. His thigh muscles wouldn't stop trembling. Watching other people glide past in their pedaloes, you would never guess how heavy those things were. The reflection of the midday sun on the crests of the waves was unbearable. Even though he wore dark glasses, all Louis could see was incandescent white. He had never liked the sun and the sun had never liked him. He hated this island and the people on it, imbecile islanders and grotesque tourists. For a week now, he had been burning his nose, his shoulders, his thighs, in close proximity to the holidaymakers who were dazed by day, hysterical by night. It had been a week of humiliations patiently borne because of the focal point – the white boat belonging to Alice's parents.

Louis felt his heartbeat return to normal and his leg muscles finally relax. The only sounds were the lapping of the water that was as clear as in a travel advertisement, and the laughter of the people picnicking on the rocks, on the beach, or in other boats. Louis stood up and placed both hands on the shell of the enormous white egg that was swaying gently. Someone had just tossed melon skins off the bridge. He watched them float away like little gondolas. Alice's parents had finished lunch. Now they would move to the front of the boat. That was their routine every day. Louis had been watching them since he'd arrived. At eight o'clock, they left the port of Pothia and went to anchor a few inlets away for the day. Of course, Louis also knew their house, as pretty as a postcard, blue and white, with flowers exactly where they should be and a stunning view across the bay, very isolated. It could have taken place there, but Louis thought the boat was better. Alice and he had had such a good time in that house, barely a year ago. But the boat, on the other hand, he had never liked. He had been out on it once or twice in the beginning, to charm Alice's father, but as that had never worked, he had quickly found good reasons not to set foot on it again. Why had that man never liked him? Louis didn't mind him, even though he thought him an absolute cretin. It's perfectly possible to like morons; they also need affection, in fact more than most ... But Louis had no money and Alice's father could accept nothing from a poor man, not even friendship; it just wasn't done. It would probably be more difficult to kill someone who didn't like you.

Noiselessly, he tied his pedalo to the rope ladder and climbed the rungs one by one. His damp feet left little haloes on the wood, which the heat immediately erased. The two old people were taking their siesta under the blue awning. They looked like two smoked chickens. There was a smell of Ambre Solaire, salt and melon. The rocking of the boat was imperceptible but even so it made him seasick, or maybe it was that music, a salsa, coming from a boat in the distance. Louis was less than two metres from them, but he hadn't given any thought as to how he was going to kill them. He'd forgotten, which was stupid; he couldn't really explain it. He hadn't brought a bludgeon, or a rope, or a knife or a gun. He'd only got as far as working out how he would get near them, as if his mere presence could kill them. Suddenly Alice's mother sat up. A fly was caught in her hair. As she shooed it away, she saw Louis over her dark glasses. Curiously, no sound escaped her. She put her hand over her naked breasts, two poor flaccid, wrinkled things. Her husband beside her had not moved. He was asleep, his arm across his eyes. Louis tried an embarrassed little smile.

'Louis? What are you doing here?'

Louis put a finger to his lips and signalled to her to come with him. Alice's mother hesitated a moment, wrapped herself in a towel, rose and followed him to the back of the boat.

'Is Alice with you? Why didn't you tel—'

'Let's go down to the cabin. Come on, please.'

It was unbearably hot. Alice's mother stopped at the foot of the stairs to adjust her towel.

'Louis, are you going to explain what's going on?'

Louis looked desperately round him; there were kitchen knives and bottles. The most anodyne of objects could become a weapon. That large cushion, for example.

'Louis, what are you doing? Lou—'

He rushed at her, threw her down on the bunk, the cushion jammed over her face. One by one the old lady's false nails broke against Louis's shoulders without doing him the slightest damage. The almost naked body struggling under his gave him an incredible erection. He leant with all his weight on the cushion. This lasted until a large red cloud burst in his head and in his swimming trunks, then everything went soft, damp and sticky. With a last jerk, the old woman knocked a table lamp to the floor where it shattered.

'Éliane? Éliane, what's going on?'

Louis dived into the dark corner at the foot of the stairs and seized a bottle by its neck. The hurried footsteps on the bridge above his head made his heart stand still. Alice's father appeared, bald head first, then his shoulders, covered in long grey hair. Louis hit him with all his strength, closing his eyes. The old man let out a raucous cry and fell to his knees, his hands on his head, covered in blood. He moaned like a child. Louis hit him with the bottle again, but the hands were like a helmet. The man was curled up on the floor kicking his feet. It was impossible to get his hands away from his head as he kicked. Blood had made everything slippery. And it was so narrow! Louis felt as if he were fighting in a cupboard; he couldn't raise his arm high enough to deliver a fatal blow to the old man who was letting out strangled cries. He let the bottle fall and squeezed the old man's throat, feeling the tendons and soft skin rolling under his fingers. Finally his mouth opened, with its displaced dentures, and his eyes bulged in terror, the corneas a bluish white. It was over. Louis couldn't unclench his hands. They stayed in the shape of the man's neck as he sat on the edge of the bunk and placed them on his thighs. He felt as if his head had been under the large bell of Notre Dame. All this blood, viscous, everywhere on his body; he wanted to cry, like a newborn. But instead of that, he urinated, without even getting up, and if his guts hadn't been all knotted up, he would have defecated as well.

In life, everything hinged on a matter of seconds; the merest millimetre could make the difference between success and failure.

13

'It was over in the space of a second. I didn't even think about it. She was a metre from the window. It all happened in one movement: I took her by the waist, as if to make her dance, and threw her out of the window, not maliciously, but as if she was a thing, a dead plant.'

As he tells me his story, Christophe knits his brow, like a child struggling in class.

'It was so easy ... one second she was there and the next she was gone from the room, gone from life, and I'd only had to move her a metre ...'

'Then what?'

'Then, nothing. I went downstairs, saw her body at the bottom of the building lying almost in the shape of a swastika, arms and legs all over the place. I got into my car and drove away.'

'And you didn't see anybody? ... Nobody saw you? ... She didn't scream?'

'No, I don't think so. I didn't even hear her body hit the pavement. Everything was quiet, or at least it seemed so ... This is going to sound really clichéd, but it was as if I was dreaming. Even afterwards, when I took the kids round to my parents', even in the car on the way here, even now talking to you. I can't be sure I'm really here.'

No wonder. I'm even beginning to doubt this peaceful Normandy beach is real. What a funny place to come to tell me you've just defenestrated your mother-in-law ... The plus side of all this is that Christophe's problems make mine pale into insignificance. Imagine Hélène turning up or my dear editor calling to chase me about something – before they even had a chance to start berating me, I'd tell them something to shut them up: 'Sorry, my friend has just murdered his mother-in-law.' That's right, the tall, kind-eyed gentleman sitting beside me and getting his arse damp on the wet sand is a murderer, a real one! This is in a whole different league from Louis's crimes, gory or otherwise, crimes on paper, petty offences that leave only ink on your hands. As for Christophe, he really killed the old bird, bish, bash, bosh, just like he said: a little dance step and off she goes, straight out of the window! ... I feel like a little kid beside him. Why spend all this time trying to think up stories? I want him to tell me his, over and over, in more and more detail.

'But why ... I mean, did she say something to you? Were you planning to do it when you went over there?'

'No, I just wanted to talk to her about Nane's childhood, see some pictures of her when she was little. She said it was late, that I should call tomorrow.'

'The old bitch!'

'No, why? She looked tired; she didn't say it in a nasty way. She lit a cigarette and turned towards the open window.'

'She had her back to you?'

'Yes. She adjusted her dressing gown and shivered, choking back a sob, moving awkwardly. It's true it wasn't warm, but the window was wide open. I realised she was the one taking her leave, not me. It was like chucking away a fag end, she was so light … Have you seen that seagull?'

'Which one?'

'The big grey one. It's only got one leg.'

'You think?'

'Yes, just the one.'

The big grey bird hobbles at a distance from the others. As soon as it tries to approach the group, they all start pecking it and ruffling their feathers to drive it away. The sky behind them looks like the closing credits of a film.

'So what are you going to do now? Turn yourself in? Run off to Rio?'

'I don't know, I haven't thought about it yet. I'm a bit afraid of the police. Which isn't the way it should be, really.'

'Take your time. You can stay here as long as you like.'

'Thanks. How come Hélène's not here?'

'Work problems in Paris.'

'She was asking me the other day if I'd seen Nat.'

'Shall we go back? I'm freezing my balls off out here.'

'Yes … Do you remember last year, with the kids? We had a laugh, didn't we? You made such a mess of the barbecue …'

'Yes, we had a laugh. Come on, it's cold.'

Christophe stretches out his long limbs, taps his shoes together to get the sand off. The sun has left a huge bruise on the sky.

'Hey, look at that! A nautilus! I've never found one as good as that here.'

Christophe shows me a magnificent fossil, much nicer than any I've collected nearby. The hanged man gets all the luck.

We get home to find Nathalie giggling on the phone.

'OK, David, see you tomorrow.' She says 'bye' in English, then hangs up. 'That was my boyfriend David, from Rouen. I'm going to see him tomorrow. I got pizzas – fancy some?'

This David sounds like a right little shit.

14

The hardest thing was getting the blood out from under his nails. There were still a few traces under his left thumbnail and the nail of the little finger on his right hand. The rest had dissolved in the infinite memory of the Mediterranean. Louis didn't remember a thing, just a vague headache, that's all. He worked patiently at the little brown stain under his left thumbnail with the corner of a cigarette packet. He had nothing else to do as he waited for the plane to take him back to Paris. All around him suntanned tourists milled about in flip-flops and frayed Bermudas. The airport resembled a works canteen. At a neighbouring table a group of French people were swapping anecdotes, which they would rehash in the winter when they looked back nostalgically on their holidays. Someone said, 'Apparently it was fourteen degrees in Paris this morning!' A disappointed clamour followed that announcement. Louis hoped it would be raining when they arrived, a little drizzle, normal weather. He wanted to get back to his caravan and not see anyone for a while, at least no one he knew. Alice would probably telephone him; he wouldn't answer. He did not wish to hear about the horrific, incomprehensible death of her parents. You die as you live; the choice is made a long time ago, just as you choose to come out of one belly instead of another. The important thing was that they were dead, that Alice would now inherit, that she would be sheltered from hardship and that it was he, Louis, who had gifted her this radiant and unexpected future. But, God, the old bloke put up a fight! Louis's fingers tensed at the memory of Alice's father's dry, sinewy neck.

'Would you like a nail file?'

'Excuse me?'

'You'll never manage with your piece of card. Here ...'

A woman of indeterminate age (forty-five? Seventy?) held out a pocket nail file between two coral-polished nails.

'Thanks. It's rust; it won't come off.'

'I know what that's like – I ruined a brand-new pair of trousers on the boat, the first day I wore them! It's awful, rust, and yet, it's very beautiful. Do you sail?'

'No, not often. This is from the balcony rail at my hotel. There, it's gone, thank you.'

The particle of dried blood drifted down to the floor, dust to dust. At the other end of the waiting area, an employee was vacuuming. Louis and the lady watched him for a moment, then they caught each other's eye. They smiled at one another. A thousand little wrinkles appeared around the lady's eyes.

'That's where everything ends up, in a vacuum-cleaner bag.'

Louis wasn't quite sure that was what she had said, but that's what he heard. He made a vague hand gesture that could have meant anything and lit a cigarette. He was embarrassed by the woman, but attracted at the same time. Everything she said seemed to have a double meaning. She was contradictory – old but at the same time young, like two overlaid images.

'Could I have one?'

'Yes, of course! How rude of me ...'

As he bent forward to give her a light, Louis received a waft of violet perfume full in the face. The woman barely had any cleavage, but it was touching. Somewhere inside the skin sagging around that neck there was a young girl. Because she wore a grey silk turban, it was impossible to tell what colour her hair was. Judging by her eyebrows, it was black. But could you accept the evidence of such well-drawn eyebrows?

'I gave up smoking yesterday.'

'Well done!'

'It was easy – it's just a question of will power.'

They both laughed, and relaxed. Louis, especially,

felt less tense. Good vibrations wove themselves around them.

'Where were you staying?'

'Kalymnos.'

'So was I! Funny that we didn't bump into each other.'

'I wasn't there for long.'

They then exchanged banalities, as you do with strangers. 'I used to have a little dog called Fidji ... I had an absolutely awful Christmas ... Lille is a very pleasant city ... I don't like going to the cinema, I prefer watching television ... During the war, I was living in Le Var, I was twelve ...' etc.

Passengers for flight 605 to Paris ...

'Ah, that's us!'

Of course, by the most enormous coincidence they found themselves seated beside each other.

'I'm Marion.'

'Louis, so pleased to meet you.'

They fastened their seat belts. The plane took off. The ground was marbled with white clouds. The sea was now no more than a pond. Marion's hands were like old silk and she wore three rings, but no wedding band.

'Do you have children, Marion?'

'Children? Goodness me, no, I never married. Why?'

'Oh, no reason.'

15

'It's funny – the way you're talking about it, anyone would think you were jealous of him.'

'Me, jealous of Christophe?'

'Yes, you; it's like you're wishing it was you in the shit instead of him.'

I had to turn to face the wall, muttering, 'Don't be stupid, I've got enough shit of my own to deal with.' But the truth is, Nathalie's right. I'd never admit it, but I've always been jealous of Christophe. From when we were very little, when we played football together and he was the goalie. I'd have liked to go in goal – no way, I was far too small. I can see him now, after school, on the patch of wasteland that we used as our pitch for everything. He'd put his jacket down, count four steps and then drop his satchel. He was totally at home between the goalposts; nothing got past him. He had gloves too. Later, I envied the love he shared with Nane, the pain he felt when she left him, the way he cared for his children, his exemplary approach to Nane's illness, the crap shoes he bought at André and yes, of course, the glorious act he had just committed.

He lives, I bluff; he's a magician, I'm a con artist; he touches, I manipulate. I can't think about him without comparing myself to him. The fact of the matter is he has always put the spotlight on my own mediocrity. It doesn't stop me loving him; in fact it's probably why I do.

In the end, we just had to get on and do it, Nat and me. So many awkward moments! Faced with such firm flesh, breasts and buttocks as hard as tennis balls, it was like having a blank page put in front of me, and scrawling all over it. I felt as if I was putting on a new item of clothing; I'm used to squidgier skins, more practised and therefore more practicable. She must have been taken aback at my shyness. What had she expected?

I didn't even hear her leave this morning. She left a note on the bedside light: 'I'll call you tonight x.' Her mother leaves me notes everywhere too. 'See you tonight xxx. Don't forget to pick up the dry cleaning xxx. There's an escalope in the fridge xxx.'

Downstairs, Christophe is moving pots around. I'll wait as long as I can before going down, until half past maybe. Someone's knocking at the door ... Christophe goes to answer it ... I bet it's Arlette ... What did I tell you! ... They're talking but I can't hear what they're saying ... Christophe's coming up the stairs ...

'Are you awake?'

'Ugh ... yes.'

'It's your neighbour. She wants to speak to you.'

'Sod that.'

'I think it's important.'

I can tell he's smelt Nathalie's perfume. I get out of bed, blushing. He looks at me like a guy who's just walked into the ladies' toilets. Arlette's waiting for me on the doorstep. She has a raincoat on her back and a ridiculous transparent plastic thing over her shampooed-and-set hair. It's raining.

'I'm sorry to bother you but it's Louis. The doctor came and I have to go and get some medicine. I'm afraid to leave him by himself, so if you could stay with him just while I nip to the chemist's ...'

Everything is trembling as she speaks, her cheeks, the tight curls of her hair, the raindrops along the edge of her hood. She looks like a stump of candle wax.

'Of course, Madame Vidal. I'll just put an anorak on.'

On the pavement, I ask her what the doctor said.

'Oh, you know what doctors are like! They use all these words no one understands, but I could see from his face that it was bad.'

Death is yellow, and smells of vanilla. I got a great whiff of it as I entered Louis's room. I'd like a pair of pyjamas like his, blue-and-white-striped flannelette ones with a darker blue edging around the collar and cuffs. I can't bring myself to look at the murky puddles of his eyes. His mouth sends out a few bubbles of soapy washing-up water and his chicken-skin hands quiver before resting flat against the sheet. I have no idea what to say to him: 'Feeling a bit poorly, are we, Monsieur Vidal?' Or 'Hey, Loulou, how's it hanging?' I make do with smiling like a plaster saint.

'Righto, I'll leave you boys to it … I shan't be long. Are you sure you don't want anything, Louis dear? … No, all right then, I'll be off. See you soon.'

She chokes back a sob as she leaves the room. I pull up a chair and sit beside the bed. Louis looks as if he's struggling to place me. He doesn't look afraid, just surprised by everything.

'Lovely pair of pyjamas you've got there, Monsieur Vidal.'

His mouth flares open like an old hen's arsehole, but very little comes out, so he follows up by trying to point at something over my left shoulder. I turn round to look. There's the window hung with two lace curtains depicting two peacocks facing one another. Nothing else but the raindrops zigzagging across the window panes.

'Awful weather! Not a good day for a walk.'

This is clearly not the answer he was looking for. Louis keeps pointing to the window with his trembling finger. I stand up and part the curtains.

'Oh! Look, it's my house! … Funny seeing it from here – it doesn't look like the same house at all.'

The bathroom light is on – Christophe must be

having his shower. What's he thinking? Has he come to a decision? Is he disappointed in me for sleeping with Nathalie? ... Maybe he's just looking for a towel. Either way, it won't occur to him for a second that I'm watching him from a dying man's window. Louis has completely forgotten I'm here; he's staring open-mouthed at a corner of the mahogany chest of drawers. It must be an extraordinary piece of furniture to merit such close attention. The poor old thing won't get to enjoy his new TV for long. Another one who thought himself immortal. And he'd have been right, until yesterday, or the day before. He could buy himself a TV, plan to invite his daughter to come for Easter, think about having a word with the idiot plumber who did a shoddy job of fixing his boiler, consider having a look round the shops in Caen with Arlette on Saturday ... That's over now; time is standing still for him.

Funnily enough, I found a few words written on the back of the note Nat left me this morning: 'Next Sunday, Louis went to ...' – something I must have scribbled down for my book. I have no idea where 'my' Louis was supposed to go, or had gone, but the clash of future and past in the sentence gave me the impression of seeing double. Like Monsieur Vidal, I felt as if I was on standby, not in the past, future, or present. The present is where other people are. Nat, who's bounding along the platform at Rouen station to throw herself into the arms of a cocky little blond boy;

Hélène, who's biting her nails and drinking coffee amid a sea of printed papers; Christophe, drying his hair and wondering whether or not to hand himself in to the police; Madame Vidal, loading her shopping basket with bottles and tubes of medicine as expensive as they are pointless … I return to my seat. If you're going to be nowhere, you may as well do it sitting down. But I don't stay there long. Arlette pushes the door open, smiling weakly, shrouded in a wet mist.

'I wasn't too long, was I? There was a queue at the chemist's but Monsieur Langlois let me go first. I got you a piece of calves' liver; you can eat that on its own … What? What do you want?'

Monsieur Vidal is pointing at the window again, opening and closing his mouth like a fish.

'You want me to turn the heating up? … There you go.'

While Madame Vidal turns the knob on the radiator beneath the window, Monsieur Vidal looks at me with disgust as if to say, 'See, muggins, it wasn't that hard, was it?'

'Right, Madame Vidal, Louis, I'd better be off …'

'Of course. I'll see you out.'

Before opening the front door:

'So, how does he seem to you?'

'Oh, you know, I'm no doctor. He's obviously tired, but … this weather doesn't help, sunny one day, horrible the next. It wears you down.'

She doesn't seem entirely satisfied with my diagnosis. Still, I could hardly reply, 'If he was a used car, he'd be unsellable.'

'Anyway, if you need anything, don't hesitate.'

'That's kind of you. I've called my daughter. She'll be here on Sunday; she can't come any sooner.'

Arlette can see from the way I'm dancing from one foot to the other that I'm itching to leave, and I escape out of the door as the first gust of wind blows in. Halfway between the Vidals' house and mine, I stop and take a detour towards the café without a name. I feel like a beer and a cigarette. By the time I arrive I'm as damp and smelly as a mouldy old sponge. The couple who own the place are the only people there. I drink two halves in quick succession. The owner tells his wife he should have taken the opportunity to repaint the shutters last weekend. She doesn't respond; she's hunched over the needlepoint she's working on, depicting the head of a German shepherd. He should have spoken to me about it – I bet I'd have loads to say on the subject of his shutters. I feel as though I could talk convincingly on any topic. I down a third half and walk back up Rue de la Mer, now as washed out as an old theatre set.

Christophe is doing last night's washing up. I give him a brief account of my visit to the old couple next door, and ask him if he's all right. Yes, he slept better than ever and is all the calmer for it. Hélène rang –

she's around until lunchtime. And then Madame Beck called about urgent corrections on a book. He's thinking of going for a quick stroll down to the beach. Yes, even in this weather. He needs some air; he won't be gone long. For a moment I wonder if I should go with him, but he doesn't look like a man who's about to go and drown himself; still, those I know who've done so didn't look as if they would either. As long as he's not dead, a living person is still a living person, in the same way a criminal is still an innocent man a split second before committing his crime. I take advantage of Christophe's absence to do my telephone duties. The 'please hold' message that comes ahead of Hélène's voice annoys me even more than usual.

'Oh, it's you. Is everything OK?'

'Yes, as good as can be expected.'

'What's going on with Christophe? He said he'd done something stupid.'

'He killed Nane's mother.'

'WHAT?'

'He threw her out of the window.'

Silence. 'I don't know what to say ... What's he going to do?'

'No idea. He's gone for a walk on the beach.'

Silence. 'Do you want me to come over?'

'It wouldn't change anything. I mean, it might be better if it's just the two of us, me and him.'

'Yes, I understand ... I can't believe it ... What

about you, what do you think about it all?'

'Nothing.'

'What do you mean, nothing? Haven't you told him to hand himself in? He's got mitigating circumstances after all! You should give him some advice, tell him to—'

'Listen, Hélène, it's his decision. I'm just trying to look after him. What more can I do?'

'But the longer he leaves it, the worse it will look for him!'

'Maybe … I'll talk to him when he gets back. I'll let you know.'

'Yes … What a crazy business! … And how are you taking it all?'

'Oh, you know, so-so.'

'OK, well, I've got a meeting in five minutes … Oh, no news of Nat?'

'Er, yes, she phoned and said she's in Rouen with a friend, David – ring any bells?'

'Yes, he was at school with her last year. Did she say when she's planning on coming home?'

'No, she said she was thinking of coming here tomorrow.'

'And you said yes? … With Christophe there?'

'He's not a professional killer.'

'That's not what I meant. If you'd rather I didn't come, I don't see why you'd want Nat there.'

'Well, you know, I didn't really think about it. I've

got other things on my mind. She'll stay over and I'll send her off the next morning. Anyway, there's nothing to say she won't change her mind in the meantime.'

'Yes, knowing her … OK, I'd better go. Love you, take care of yourself. Give me a call tonight.'

How far away she seems … ever further away. I could have been in England with her now; there would have been no Nat, no Christophe, no Vidals. There's no place to hide.

16

Marion lived in an artist's studio in the eighteenth arrondissement, in an artists' commune inhabited by people like her who were not artists. Everything in it was white, including the cat. It was the third time since they'd returned from Greece that Louis had come to see her. He already had his allotted place – the right-hand seat of the white fake-leather sofa opposite the window diffusing a light that was … white. It was four o'clock and they were drinking a deliciously cold rosé champagne. The day was heavy, so the air in the studio was stultifying. The rare breaths of air were like blasts from a hairdryer. There were crowds of people in the street, all still in holiday mode. In the bus on the way, girls pulled their skirts up to their thighs and fanned themselves with magazines. They were like ripe figs. The men, with their leaden complexions, their shirts sticking to them and their ties pulled sideways, sat looking vacant, their mouths open. People seemed to pass for no obvious reason from a state of torpor to feverish agitation, akin to hysteria. When he arrived at Marion's you could have wrung him out, like a mop.

They were at that delicious stage in their relationship when they told each other everything without ever giving anything away, as you do when you meet a stranger on the train. You allow yourself to lie by adding an element of truth, or tell the truth with a few lies thrown in, lying having the indisputable superiority of being infinitely adaptable.

'You were a teacher? That must have been terrible!'

'It was! Look ...'

Marion put a pair of spectacles on the end of her nose and stared at Louis severely.

'What did you teach the children? Was it things like "I before E except after C"?'

'Yes and worse!'

'It's criminal to put things like that in children's heads.'

'We're there to make them into adults; we wipe out childhood.'

'I never liked school. I always found it humiliating to be made to learn things I didn't know.'

Marion took the spectacles off and poured two more glasses of champagne. She was still very tanned. Even in winter she would look as if she were on holiday. Louis tried to imagine her a few years younger. He preferred her as she was, wearing her wrinkles like family jewels.

'Even in glasses, I can't see you as a schoolteacher.'

'Yet I was one and I didn't wear glasses then. Does that disappoint you?'

'Is that why you never had any children?'

'Perhaps.'

They drank in silence. The purring of the cat spiralled up and back down again. Louis stood up. 'Excuse me.'

The walls of the loo were covered with exotic postcards of the sea, beaches or coconut palms. Louis took one down. On the back: 'Dear Marion, this is the view from our hotel. Paris is no more than a bad memory. Thinking of you often, lots of love, Chantal and Bob.'

In a week, or maybe a month, Marion would tell him about Chantal and Bob. He felt as if he'd known them for ever. Inch by inch Louis was installing himself in Marion's life and felt comfortable there. He wanted to bask in it like the white cat in the pool of light by the window. They hadn't yet made love. That would come, probably, but for now it was of no importance. And perhaps it never would be.

What was more certain was that they would sleep in each other's arms.

Louis had been evasive about his past, offering snippets about his childhood, crumbs of his existence, peppered with some fairy tales. When Marion wanted to know more, he lied, he made up a life, to please her. He had spent too much time living with women he had not been able to satisfy while he was with them. Now they were financially secure thanks to him, he could retire with no sense of guilt. Marion had a few years on him; she could teach him how to live as a pensioner. He would have moved straight from childhood to retirement without stopping at adulthood, which he was quite proud of. He and Marion would visit little provincial museums, watch daytime television, go on bateaux mouches, have Chantal and Bob over, cure their little colds, their little injuries with little attentions and gifts. That little life was the height of his ambition. Louis had been born for old age, he had always known that.

In an hour he would be meeting Alice, probably for the last time. She had just returned from Greece where her parents had been buried. She was the one who had called him, she needed to speak to him. He couldn't see what she had to say to him, unless it was thank you, but obviously she wouldn't do that because she didn't know and would never know that she owed her providential inheritance to him. In any case, no one was overjoyed at the death of their parents, at least not immediately, especially when they had been killed in a hideous, inexplicable crime. He would see Alice one last time and Marion would replace Alice, as Alice had replaced Agnès, because everyone was replaceable, discardable, just like him. Louis buttoned himself up and checked to make sure he hadn't left any drops around the toilet. Everything was so clean here.

In the main room, Marion was on all fours playing with the cat.

'I have to go out, Marion, I have a meeting at six o'clock. But before I go, I wanted to ask you if you'll marry me?'

'Marry you? What on earth for?'

'I don't know, I think it would be good.'

'It's very unexpected. Do you love me?'

'I could. I'll call you tomorrow. Would you like to take a trip on a bateau mouche if the weather's good?'

He wanted to say to her, 'Alice! Alice! Look how happy everyone around you is. They're coming out of the cinema, or else they're on their way in. They all have parents, maybe are parents themselves. They're all mortal, but they don't know it yet, they're just happy to be here, to laugh while they can. You feel like an orphan now, but you're finally going to be yourself, without owing anyone anything. Perhaps that's what you don't like?'

Alice was very beautiful, much more beautiful than the last time he'd seen her by the ponds. She was wearing clothes he didn't recognise, chic, sober and brand new.

'That suit looks really good on you. Very smart.'

'You think so? I didn't have anything suitable to wear for the funeral.'

She blushed, instinctively turning to look at her reflection in the café window, one hand ruffling her hair. A quick smile, and then the mask of grief was back in place.

'So, what are you going to do now you are rich?'

'I don't know ... Buy a flat. You say that as if I'd just won the lottery. My parents are dead, for Christ's sake! Murdered!'

'I'm sorry, I—'

'No, it's my fault. It's just this is all so unbelievable; everything's happening so quickly! But what about you, what have you been up to recently? I tried to call you dozens of times – you were never there ... Aren't you going to ask me for news of the children?'

'Yes, yes, of course. How are they?'

'You don't give a stuff ... You don't care about anything; I don't know who you are any more. Is there still anything between us?'

Apart from a table and two empty glasses, Louis couldn't think of a single thing between them. He had never realised before how similar she was to Agnès.

'Have ... have you met someone else? That's it, there's someone else. Is there someone else?'

She was like someone knocking on the door of an empty house. Louis shrugged.

He thought back to that autumn. He had gone to meet Agnès at her dance class. He had known Alice for six months. The class was at the youth club in Colombes. He didn't normally go there, but this once, because it was his birthday and she had prepared a surprise for him, she had insisted that he was not to arrive at the house before her. Fred was a year old; he was staying with his grandparents. It was already dark, quite cold. Colombes station was like a rusty cage. The street that led to the youth club was a gloomy passageway in spite of the shops and neon lights, a Champs-Élysées for dwarfs. He had had to ask the way several times, having got lost in alleyways with ridiculously puffed-up names. But he had still arrived early and been forced to watch the dire dance efforts of Agnès and her friends on their rubber mats. Seeing him leaning against a wall, she gave what was meant to be an elegant little wave, but was actually excruciating. She looked like a seal climbing out of water. The smell of chalk, hot rubber and feet made him feel nauseous. He had turned away. A badly printed poster announced the dates of various events: a singer from Languedoc, the Myrian Pichon ballet dancers, a table-tennis tournament, a production of *Ubu roi* and a judo competition. He heard the stamping of feet on the floor and the raucous voice of the teacher, 'Point your toes, point!'

In the train on the way back, everything seemed tired and poverty-stricken. Sometimes, as if by chance, Agnès's mouth sought Louis's, and, as if by chance, he avoided it. Then they were on the metro, the steps of the building, at the front door where Agnès said, 'Close your eyes! You can open them when I tell you to.' He would have liked never to open them because he knew what he would see: the kitchen table in the middle of the room, adorned with their sole tablecloth, three or four wilting carnations in a vase, two candles in front of two plates with serviettes, and, under his, a lighter or a pen. Behind his eyelids, all he could see was Alice, with whom he had spent the day. But he'd had to open his eyes and exclaim in delight, 'Oh! A lighter!'

As he stood at the window, glass in hand, listening to Agnès busying herself in the kitchen, he spotted that ageless-seeming woman that everyone called Maria on the other side of the courtyard. She had been struck down with an incurable illness; a port-wine stain covered three-quarters of her face, ending in a pool under her chin. It was monstrous. She was brushing her hair, slowly, with coquettish gestures, arranging a curl here and there, carefree and terribly beautiful.

When Agnès came out of the kitchen, he couldn't explain why he was crying. The next morning he left.

17

'But it's spoken language, Madame Beck! Kids say, "I dunno, I'm gonna, I ain't" … In the text, maybe, but not in the dialogue … Fine, look, Madame Beck, take them all out. Just send me my cheque, that's all I ask … That's right. Now excuse me but I've got a whole heap of corpses to get back to … Of course, Madame Beck. Goodbye, Madame Beck.'

My editor's whinging voice has left the telephone all sticky. It was coming through the little holes in the handset like meat from a butcher's mincer. Very unsavoury. Christophe returned from the beach shrouded in mist while Madame Beck was breaking my balls with her idiot grammar. He looked like a baby who'd just had a bath. He brought back a bottle of Burgundy and a good slab of brawn.

'What's up?'

'Just the editor saying "na-na-na-na-na". They're like nits – harmless but irritating. You all right?'

'Yes. The wind outside's incredible. Makes you want to fly a kite. Fancy a snack?'

He opens the bottle and we tuck in to the brawn straight from the paper it's wrapped in, bearing a picture of a jolly little dancing pig in a hat waving a string of sausages: 'Charcuterie Bénoult, world-champion tripe and black pudding maker'. Still chewing, Christophe starts taking the shells and pebbles he's collected for the children from his pockets. He spreads them out on the table and puts them in size order. He tells me that when he was little, he used to love playing with his grandmother's button collection. There were buttons of every type, made of wood, horn, mother-of-pearl, leather, fabric … He would plunge his hands into the box like a pirate revelling in a chest of gold coins. Then he would put them in order, make families or armies of them. He'd spend hours at it. Do I remember his grandmother? Vaguely, built like a tank with a bun on top?

Yes! And she put loads of butter on our bread? That's the one! Christ, yes, she slathered it on thick! Fat's a symbol of wealth, for common people. For instance, she would always ask the butcher for fatty veal for her blanquette, because it had a better flavour. It's true there's nothing like a bit of fat in cold weather, and a glass of Burgundy too. The glasses are drained and refilled. Take the Eskimos, for example, they eat nothing but fat; they couldn't survive otherwise. Not silly, Eskimos.

The opportunity is too good to pass up – I seize it

with both hands. No, the Eskimos are damn well not silly! After all, aren't they the ones who've found the best possible solution for getting their elderly off their hands? Sit them on a chunk of ice, give it a kick and off they go – bon voyage! Christophe thinks for a moment, holding the glass to his lips. He doesn't seem to entirely approve of my tale of old people drifting off on an ice floe, probably because of his grandma. He prefers the Native American formula whereby granddad leaves the tribe to go and die with dignity beneath a venerable pine tree at the top of a mountain. I point out that if we were to expect the same thing of ours, we'd probably draw a blank as the fucking doctors have made them practically immortal. He admits I'm right, but even so, back in the days we looked after our elderly, they lived with their children until the end. I go 'Ha ha ha!' as if I learnt to laugh from a bad book. Their children! They can't even put up with each other, let alone with the elderly thrown in! No, I'm telling you the Eskimos have the cleanest answer. Also, this Sioux thing you're talking about, it's not a million miles from suicide, and that's frowned upon in our religions; with my system of not-quite-murder, you're sending them on a fast train to paradise. Am I right or am I right? Christophe shakes his head, looking doubtful. The wine makes me as pig-headed as a missionary. I won't drop it: Nane's mother had a place in hell with her name on it, but you sent her to heaven.

'Well, I obviously didn't put my back into it, since she fell down to earth again immediately.'

Christophe drains his glass and smiles.

'Wanna know what Grégoire told me the other day, when I picked him up from school? What do you get when a Chinaman jumps off the Eiffel Tower? ... A chink in the pavement!'

I never get jokes, but I can't seem to resist this one. It feels so good to laugh for the sake of it, a favour we should do ourselves more often. I make a note: 'Don't forget to laugh over silly stuff.' I empty the last of the bottle into our glasses, two purple tears.

'Hey, if we're going to want another one, we should go now – the shops will soon be shut until four.'

'It's going to be one of those days then, is it?'

'It may well be.'

Outside, the wind carries us to Coccinelle so that we barely need to walk. While we're paying for our two bottles (one would not have sufficed) at the till of the mini-market, I tell Christophe I am determined not to put up with any more crap in my life. Editors, money, girls, winter, sick to death of all of it! Every day could be summer if we wanted it to be – it's up to us; we could leave, skedaddle, get the hell out!

On the way home, holding the bottles under my arms, head down against the icy wind, I describe to him in great detail the pleasures of a game of pétanque under the plane trees: the blue shadows, the speckles of light on skin that smells of salt and sun, bare feet in sandals ...

'I don't like sandals. They dig into your feet and make you look like an idiot.'

'OK, fine, no sandals. But think about it – smoking a nice fat spliff leaning against a cypress tree, the peppery smoke from the weed mingling with the fragrance of thyme and lavender ...'

'A nice fat spliff – now you're talking ...'

'I know a guy in Rouen. We could go later, if you like.'

The house smells of wet dog and toilets. It takes a monumental effort to remain standing.

'Shit! Are we really going to wait until our beards have grown down to our knees before we go and find our place in the sun? You have to ride the wave when you catch it. I know a little place in Greece where you can live for nothing; a bit of bread and cheese, a few figs ...'

'Is there no way of turning the heating up? Even my teeth are cold.'

'No, it's on maximum, but don't worry, Granddad, let's make ourselves a nice poor man's soup with what's left in the house. Pour us a drink, would you.'

You have to keep your hands busy, get back in touch with your body, to avoid becoming trapped by the ice. I take a stock pot out of the cupboard and throw in everything I can lay my hands on: carrots, lentils, an old yellowed leek, some Gruyère, a handful of pasta. I have ten arms, ten legs; I spread myself star-shaped across all four corners of the kitchen. I've put on the uniform of Captain Ahab; the white whale is right here, in a corner of my head. Meanwhile, in Christophe's head there's nothing but weariness, with bars across it and little kids passing through oranges. Now's the time to be an artist, a real one, a shaman, to move aside and make room for him. There is no better way of getting a man to share his troubles than by talking about one's own. In this case, all I have to do is think about my first wife while peeling an onion.

'Do you remember Odile? Before we broke up, I heard her chatting to her friends on the phone, talking about us as if she was describing an incurable disease: things are going better ... things are much the same ... things are getting worse ... She knew I was listening – our place was so small ... Afterwards she would hang up with a sigh, cracking her knuckles because she knew I couldn't stand it. I'd tell her, "You're squeaking like a new shoe" ... It went on like that for more than a year. We didn't think we'd ever get over it. I bumped into her six months ago. She was doing fine, and so was I. People are pretty solid, really, aren't they?'

'I'd say more soluble.'

'OK, soluble, then. Have you finished with the carrots?'

'I can't do it. They're all floppy.'

Jesus, he's a tough nut to crack! I can't squeeze the slightest tear out of him. I turn the screw, tell him about the little girl on the news, clutching a beam and slowly becoming mired in a river of mud. Then I go on to the stories my mother told me to send me to sleep, the fire at the Bazar de la Charité, the raft of the *Medusa* and the absurd death, three years later, of one of the sole survivors, the shipwright Corréard, who drowned in a puddle, pissed, on his way home from a country dance. And the *Titanic*! Ah, the *Titanic*! ... And that toothache I had last year! In agony for an entire Sunday, I was! Ooh, I can still feel it now ... Awful!

'So anyway, this soup of yours ...'

'What about it?'

'I can't smell anything.'

No wonder – I've forgotten to put the gas on underneath it.

'Look, it's not worth crying about. It doesn't matter.'

Oh but it does! I can't even make a nice hot soup for my old friend the murderer who's dying of cold. I break down, unable to speak, hanging off the edge of my chair as if teetering on the edge of the world, my feet swinging in the void.

Out of the corner of my red eye, peering between the now empty bottles, I watch my Christophe suck in all the air in the room, stand up straight and become once again what he has always been, Saint Christopher carrying the little children who are afraid of getting their feet wet.

'Right, come on, we're going to Rouen to get some weed. A bit of fresh air will do us good. I'm not cold any more; everything's fine.'

I've worked my magic, but at a price.

'All right, I'll puke and then we can go.'

We take Christophe's car, an Opel as solid and reliable as him, although the seats are a little on the firm side. He takes the wheel – he's always handled his drink better than me. What's the point of drinking if not to get drunk? Plus I like being ferried around by other people. The windscreen wipers are slightly out of time with the music coming from the radio, a Dalida song: 'He had just turned eighteen, he was beautiful like a child, strong like a man ...' It's making my head throb. I don't mind; I need a headache the way a blind man needs his dog. The world outside the car is like my soup, uncooked brown mush. A few times, as we pass a police station, Christophe slows down to peer in before speeding up again.

'Do you want to hand yourself in?'

'No, I'm just looking.'

'What if we didn't stop at Rouen?'

'Then we wouldn't smoke a spliff.'

'And what if we said to hell with the spliff and all the rest of it? What if we just kept on driving?'

'Since the Earth's round, we'd end up back where we started.'

'Jesus, you're annoying sometimes! What I mean is, if we never stopped, never ever.'

'Then we'd be dead.'

'Do you think you can be dead without knowing it?'

'And you say I'm annoying? How the hell should I know? I just want to smoke a spliff, that's all.'

We're in Rouen because that's what the sign says, plus there's a cathedral and the Gros Horloge – if it wasn't for them, we could be in any European city: same town centre with the same pedestrianised streets, same little cobblestones laid like fish scales, same tubs filled with anaemic privet, same branches of Chevignon, same jeans shops, same croissant stands, same guitar strummers, same accordion players, same red-nosed clowns following you and mimicking your movements. Nowheresville. We've been wandering around for an hour; I'm lost, as lost as lost can be. Funnily enough, the last (and only) time I came to this dealer was three years ago, on a day as fuzzy as this one.

'It's definitely next to a bakery. You'll laugh, but this is exactly like last time. I came with a friend. We had a joint, then two, then three, and then, on the stroke of one in the morning, I had the urge to take a stroll around town. I went out, had a nose around, my head filled with the city stars, till my calves couldn't take anymore. Only, I'd forgotten to take his address. Imagine, in November, at two in the morning, not a rat on the streets. And even if there had been someone, what could I have said? Do you know Horatio, the guy who sells weed and lives by a bakery? Hours I spent circling around this fucking town until eventually I found him by accident.'

'I'd just like to point out that this is the third time we've passed this branch of André. We're going round in circles.'

'It's next to a bakery ...'

'There are bakeries everywhere! Come on, let's get something warm to drink; it's starting to rain.'

Through the opaque windows of the café, the road is morphing into an aquarium, clouded by the violet ink of the falling night. My Viandox tastes like a wet rag. I leave it to cool down while I watch the passers-by skip between puddles of shadow and neon, hunched over, holding newspapers open over their heads. They look like sandflies. Christophe is reading the menu – written in white paint on the window – backwards, when I catch sight of Nat, in a fit of laughter, walking by on the arm of a comma-shaped man, probably David.

'Doesn't steak hachis have an "S" on the end?'

'Why the hell should I care?'

Nat, all wet, like a kitten that's fallen into the bathtub, Nat laughing, Nat happy, without me. No matter how

I try to tell myself that there's nothing extraordinary about bumping into her like this, that the centre of Rouen isn't that big and all the ghosts in the world have the right to walk there, I feel a horrible sense of unease coming over me, the sensation of turning up at a family party without having been invited.

'What's the matter? You've gone all pale.'

'Huh? Nothing, nothing, I thought I saw someone but it wasn't him. Doesn't this Viandox stink? Or maybe it's my hands; they do smell sometimes.'

'It just smells a bit damp. You know, I don't give a shit about the weed. If you want, we can just go home.'

'No! We are not going home!'

'It's almost eight. Where do you think we can go? Something's up with you all of a sudden.'

'I don't know, but we can't go home, ever. I don't want any more of this Viandox. I want a Picon bière instead.'

'Fine, fine, we'll get a Picon bière. Waiter?'

After the Picon bière, which perked me up a bit, we got back on the road, but we didn't go home. I would rather have dropped dead. We bought some beer from a corner shop that smelt of cat piss and rancid Gruyère. Christophe took a road heading towards the sea. I felt better. Everything was behind us again. I felt as if I had just avoided something terrible. J. J. Cale was on the radio. We joined in with the chorus together: 'Cocaine!' I wriggled about in my chair trying to find something to write with in my pocket. I was thinking of Louis; I had a brilliant idea. By the time I had found a scrap of paper, it had gone, evaporated. It was a shopping list: bread, sugar, washing powder, chocolate. The last word, oil, had been crossed out. Hélène had already bought some. On the other side, I wrote, 'In six months, Louis had put on six kilos.'

18

In six months, Louis had put on six kilos and been on two aeroplanes. One to Munich, the other to Copenhagen. Marion had been dying to go to those two cities. Louis would have preferred to stay put, but how could he come up with a good reason for not wanting to go to either Munich or Copenhagen when he had nothing else to do and he and Marion were newly married? Anyway, now that all the cities in the world looked alike, travelling wasn't too bad because it didn't really feel like travelling. There were the same pedestrianised streets in the centre, the same fashions, the same exasperating music everywhere – the same everything everywhere. Except that Marion, like all tourists, did not want to be taken for a tourist, which meant interminable traipsing around rancid suburbs looking for a 'typical' little hotel or a 'charming' caff whilst lugging enormous suitcases. Having said that, the exhausting excursions didn't last more than a week and the rest of the time was spent developing photos of the mini-adventures and sticking them into an album before going back to the travel agent to fetch stacks of new brochures.

'Listen to this: "Enjoy the ultimate Royal Scotland experience. The most luxurious train in the world takes you on an unforgettable journey with views of the beautiful lochs and mountains of the Highlands. Also included are private visits to gardens, stately homes and mysterious castles with commentary from an experienced guide." What do you think of that?'

'That sounds good. Is it expensive?'

'About twenty thousand francs. Not bad.'

'We'll have to see.'

Twenty thousand francs! That was about all he had left in his account. Marion thought that Louis was not rich exactly, but comfortably off. He had been spending at the same rate as Marion, that of a relatively well-off retiree. He didn't have another mother or father he could kill off. It was a bit of a concern.

'I'm going out to buy the TV guide. Is there anything else you need?'

Once in the street, that street that he didn't like and that didn't like him, he repeated, 'I'm going out to buy the TV guide. Is there anything else you need?' several times in a row. How many sentences like that had he uttered in his life? Had he expressed anything else? And was there anything else to express? If you learnt those words in all the languages in the world, you would be able to manage in any situation.

When he bought the TV guide, he also bought a French–German dictionary to learn his magic phrase. German, because he knew how to say it in English, and the French–German dictionary was on sale. In Munich, he had once wished he'd known some German. He and Marion were walking in the Englischer Garten, a sort of Bois de Boulogne in the heart of the city, full of bicycles, dogs, and Germans in shorts or dressed like punks. They took a little walk there every day before embarking on the inescapable trips to museums in the afternoon. By the lake, a little boy had passed close by them, walking a dog on a lead (although perhaps it was the dog leading the child – it was a huge dog, completely white). A flight of ducks? A sudden movement of Marion's? Something frightened the dog and his lead became wrapped round Marion's ankles, so that she, the animal and the child who held obstinately to the leather strap ended up in the black waters of the lake. The ducks were quacking, the dog was barking, his enormous mouth wide open, Marion was shouting, 'Louis! Louis!' and curiously the child was yelling 'Taxi! Taxi!' (It was only later that Louis learnt that was the dog's name.) Louis didn't fancy saving any of them. In fact, he would happily have sunk them with stones, so unbearable was their shouting. Of course, lots of people suddenly appeared from goodness knows where. Two young men had already thrown themselves into the water. The lake was not deep, but it was full of mud. They got Marion and the child out covered in sludge but the dog had made it difficult for the rescuers and it took a while to save him. While this was going on, the people on the bank, an elderly couple wearing matching jogging suits, a young woman with a twin buggy, and a handful of punks with red coxcombs, had bombarded him with questions to which he had replied by throwing his hands up: *Nix sprachen deutsch*. He would have liked to explain to them that, contrary to appearances, he had done what he could, that is, nothing. The life he was leading now that he wasn't murdering anyone any more was boring beyond belief, and, no doubt to make up for the monotony of his days, had offered him this little spectacle that was more comic than tragic. That was the reason he hadn't moved, just as you don't climb on stage to stop Juliet from poisoning herself. But the only things he knew how to say in German were *Nix sprachen deutsch, helles bier, dunkles bier, lam, schwein, rint, links, rechts* and *gut morgen*.

As she got out of the lake, dripping from head to foot, all Marion had said was, 'Why?' Why had she been knocked into a Munich lake by a dog called Taxi, or why had Louis watched her from the bank without doing anything? But, in fact, it was a more general why, encompassing an infinity of other much more profound and essential questions, a universal why, meaning 'Why me?'

Up until that point, Louis had always considered Marion to be as eternal and inevitable as spring following winter, or as the desire to drink a lovely cold beer follows a long visit to a museum. He thought that by her side he would benefit from the same status, but this tiny fault had just given rise to a doubt. Marion was submersible and could ask herself pathetic questions like 'Why me?'

Every week when he went out to buy the TV guide, Louis treated himself to a minced meat pie at the charcuterie next to the newsagent. They were so good, even cold. As he walked along, munching his pie, Louis opened the German–French dictionary at random. *Apfel* – apple, *Hase* – hare, *Schwere* – gravity, *Schwerpunkt* – centre of gravity. That's how he could have answered Marion's why beside the lake: *Schwerpunkt* instead of brushing in vain at her clothes caked in mud.

Marion was preparing rabbit in a foil parcel when he returned. It smelt of mustard and tarragon.

'You put the blue vase down so that it was balanced on the fridge door. So when I opened the fridge, it fell on the floor.'

'*Schwerpunkt.*'

'What?'

'Nothing.'

19

Christophe is bent over his plate. Sitting opposite him, it's my face that I can see above his shoulders in the mirror behind the banquette. I look like a Corsican bandit. On escapades like this, I begin to look scruffy at an alarming rate. Time hits me like a ten-ton truck. The restaurant is practically empty; we had a hard time persuading them to serve us. In the car, I'd had the strongest craving for fried fish with white wine. There wasn't any. We had beef tournedos with a glass of red. Even though the place is called La Marine. There are sextants, compasses, telescopes, bits of rigging hanging all over the walls, but no fish on the menu. I'm disappointed. When men are unhappy, they think only of drinking and becoming sailors. I feel like going to sleep, like being cradled, but refuse to admit it.

'Why are you smiling?'

'No reason. I feel relieved.'

'Have you made a decision?'

'Yes.'

'You're going to hand yourself in, aren't you?'

'Yes.'

'I knew it! But shit, we could leave, cross the border; we can get false papers, you could send for your kids, start a brand-new life! I'm here for you, damn it! I can help you! … Why hand yourself in? Who for?'

'It's time to face facts, mate. Can you see me playing Jean Valjean with a false beard? It's a lot simpler than that.'

'Right, then. Coffee and the bill! Bish, bash, bosh, it's over!'

'This is real life! I'm not the hero of one of your fucking books! I'm not a hero of anything.'

'How do you know? You've never tried. Anyway, what do I care? Go on, you go and spend ten years behind bars making espadrilles. I'm gonna keep this going.'

'Don't be so ridiculous. I'm the one on the run, not you!'

'How would you know? You think you're the only one running away from something?'

The broom, passed expertly between our legs, brings an end to the debate.

Outside, the night unravels in trails of cloud, a few paltry stars flickering between them. I piss against the car in one long hard stream. My hands are old, my dick is old, the Opel is old and Christophe, who's waiting for me at the wheel, the oldest of them all. I collapse into the seat beside him.

'OK, here's what I think we should do. We go and watch the sun come up at Étretat – you know, where we used to take the kids, where the cliff looks like a slice of cake. And then ... and then day will have dawned.'

I just shrug my shoulders. The truth is, I couldn't care less. My bladder must be directly connected to my brain. When I emptied it, I completely emptied my head, heart and the marrow of my bones. I am a kind of tube, open at both ends, incapable of taking the slightest initiative.

The car smells of plastic, mints and a full ashtray. It's like being at the prow of a boat, the trees either side of the road fringed with grey foam in the beam of the headlights. It's so nice to follow someone who knows where he's going. I should have shadowed him since nursery school; I needn't have been me or worn myself out becoming me. The road, the night, the music, how could it all come to an end? I have the firm conviction that I was destined to live for ever.

I must have fallen asleep for quite a while. The car slows down and turns down a track. There are no more trees, just an expanse of grass flattened by the weight of the sky, heavy with static clouds. There's nothing at the end of it, and I find this nothingness more and more oppressive as the car moves towards it, slowly, even more slowly, and then stops. A fixed image. Total silence. Christophe stretches his limbs, still holding the steering wheel.

'The end of the road, the end of the night.'

His serene smile, his calm assurance, the extreme banality of what he has just said annoy me immensely.

'The end of nothing at all, that's right. Now where are we? I don't like this place; let's get out of here.'

'We've been here dozens of times. Don't be an idiot, come on. The sun's going to come up. It's amazing from the top of the cliff.'

He opens his door and the void rushes into the car with the noise of a turbine. I see him walk a few metres beyond the bonnet, bent double, the two flaps of his raincoat plastered against his legs. Here we are then; the sun will rise, our hero will receive the absolution of the raging elements and then bish, bash, bosh, off he'll go to hand himself in at the police station and it's over: violins, the end, credits roll. Or even fucking stupider: he says goodbye to me, smiling, and throws himself into the abyss like an angel, disappearing between two clouds. I bash my fist against the dashboard. The glove box opens, spewing out an old rag and a pair of glasses missing a lens. What a lousy ending, what a terrible script! I force myself out of my shell, ready to scream, 'Come on then, Christophe. Do you really have nothing more original for me?' ... but the wind pushes the words back down my throat the minute I open my mouth. If I didn't keep both hands on the door handle, it would be me getting blown away. I throw myself down on all fours, fingernails digging into the ground.

From the cliff edge, Christophe turns and motions to me to join him.

'I can't! I'm scared of heights!'

The wind bats a few words back to me: 'Come! ... lovely! ... sea!'

'No! ... you come back! ... to leave!'

He doesn't want to know. He keeps beckoning to me, with his back to the void. The idiot's going to hurt himself if he keeps waving his arms about like that. I creep towards him like an animal, screwing up my eyes, the wind grasping my face like the five fingers of an enormous hand.

'Christophe, for fuck's sake, let's go!'

'Come on, the sun's coming up, it's amazing! Give me your hand.'

So what? It comes up every fucking day. I'm cold and I've got vertigo. My fingernails dig into his wrist. He drags me to the edge, to the place where hope has almost gone, where all that's left is a sorry tuft of grass to which I cling for dear life.

'Well, isn't it wonderful?'

I only open one eye, which is more than enough. Nothing about it looks wonderful to me, only terrifying: rocks like jagged teeth, an inconceivably great drop, a pack of raging waves, pure horror under a scornful sky, vaguely tinted with a milky cloud. Paralysed by fear, I can do nothing but keep staring into the chaos. My brow is drawn downwards as if by a magnet and there below I see my body in pieces, arms and legs strewn about on the rocks. I hear a voice inside me say, 'You have never been the owner of your body, merely the tenant.' It's the voice of a witch offering a shiny red apple. A cry comes back in response, the cry of the beast within me refusing point-blank to heed the call of the abyss. I close my eyes and leap backwards. My hand jerks out of Christophe's grasp. I seem to hear a sound like the crack of a whip or the whistling of a bullet, something narrowly missing me. I don't try to work it out, I roll through the grass. The only thought in my head is the need to get away from this hole, as far away as possible. I'll never be far enough away. Keep rolling, rolling …

20

The little girl was sitting on the edge of the white sofa. She'd perched Marion's glasses on the end of her nose and was holding the Gospel according to St Thomas open at page twenty-five, the page Marion had left it open at. Louis was watching her from the other end of the sofa. She was five years old and she was bored. Her name was Mylène and she was the daughter of Marion's niece. Marion had left him to look after her for the afternoon while she went shopping. Louis had played with her non-stop and read her three little books, laborious stratagems that had dragged him painfully towards three o'clock in the afternoon. Now they were both as bored as each other and a silence that almost made you want to cry reigned in the big white room. The little girl forgot about Louis. She was playing at being Marion, imitating the way she took her glasses off and put them on again. She was saying in her baby voice, 'Hasn't there been a phone call for me today?'

Louis remembered a day spent with a parrot. He had been at the house of people he hardly knew in Belgium, a huge house stranded in the middle of muddy fields. For a reason he now couldn't remember he had been left alone in the house with the parrot, a large grey bird with a red tail. He had been immersed in Maeterlinck's *The Life of the Bee* when the noise of a cork popping out of a bottle made him jump. Then came the scraping of curtains along a curtain rail and the voice of the master of the house, recognisable by his heavy Flemish accent, then the voice of his wife, high-pitched like clinking ice cubes, and finally the dog barking, all imitated to perfection. It was unbelievably realistic, especially the master and mistress of the house. At first, Louis had been amused but as it went on he became a little uncomfortable. He felt as if he were invisible and eavesdropping on private conversations, and even as if he were witnessing an intimate domestic scene. And all by dribs and drabs, interspersed with the *pop!* of corks which seemed to indicate that his hosts were fond of a drink. In front of him, they were courteous – a little distant, stiff even – but the parrot, possibly because it thought it was alone (Louis wasn't moving in his hidden corner of the room), had just given away what went on behind closed doors. It felt indecent to witness. Louis had spent the rest of the day in his bedroom on the first floor.

He had a similar feeling of indecency as he watched the little girl imitating Marion. And curiously, as with the parrot and his owners, the girl delighted in mimicking Marion's most ridiculous flaws, tics and obsessions. For a while now he himself had started to see her only as a caricature. He had had to admit to her that he had run out of money. She hadn't made any comment; in fact she had told him not to worry about it, that she had enough for both of them. But ever since, her behaviour towards him had changed. Not a lot, just enough to nag at Louis like a loose tooth. She sought his opinion less often, telephoned her friends more, imposed her choice of television programme on him. The other day he had groaned when she had asked him whether he would prefer to be buried or cremated. He had replied that he didn't mind, that death was a story for the living and that he was going to buy the bread.

The little girl was fed up with playing at being Marion and was beginning to play about a little too close to the crystal carafes and other fragile knick-knacks that Marion had brought back from her interminable trips. The white cat had immediately picked up on the change in the child's behaviour and had gone to hide under the dresser. Louis was going to have to stir himself into action.

'Mylène, it's nearly four o'clock. Would you like a cake?'

It was strange to walk along holding the hand of a little girl, keeping to her pace. He felt awkward, at once proud but shy, vulnerable but powerful. The child was taking advantage of this by wanting everything she saw: a red motorbike, a multicoloured feather, balls, sweets. It was like having a dog on a lead that would suddenly stop in its tracks.

'That! ... I want that!'

Louis felt sick when he saw what the plump little figure was pointing at. He had completely forgotten the fair that had been set up on the other side of the boulevard. Or he would, of course, have taken the other road. For as long as he could remember he had had a horror of fairs, circuses and in general of anything where fun was obligatory. The rare memories he had of fairs comprised nothing but drunken soldiers, obese women, terrifying dwarfs, which automatically triggered a violent feeling of nausea.

'But your cake? Don't you want it any more?'

'Nooo! Want roundabouts!'

Two solutions: he could pick Mylène up, kicking and screaming, and force his way through the crowd like a child catcher and attach her to a chair when they got home, or he could give in and let himself be dragged to the fair like a lamb to the slaughter.

He had to negotiate forcefully with a little red-haired boy for the driving seat of an ambulance. Now Mylène was going round and round, fading and disappearing in a whirlwind of light. Slyly, nausea was taking hold of Louis. He breathed slowly and deeply. He must not look at the roundabout, anything but the roundabout, the sky for example … But his glance fell on the big wheel which, seen from this angle, seemed to be coming straight at him. Everywhere he tried to rest his eyes, it was all rods, gears and pistons coming to crush him. The stale smell of *frites*, waffles and toffee apples was the final straw. He had to sit down immediately or he would have collapsed in the dust amongst the fag ends, chewing gum, tickets, candyfloss sticks and crushed Coke cans. Over there, between two stalls, he thought he could make out a sort of drum, a red affair about buttock height. In spite of the crowd, he would get to that red thing, he had to. Once he was sitting on it, he closed his eyes. Three seconds more and he would have fallen over. An icy sweat broke out on his forehead and his legs wouldn't stop trembling.

'Louis?'

Louis half opened one eye. Agnès's head appeared in close-up wearing a ridiculous white cap. 'Agnès?'

'Louis! What are you doing here? Is everything OK? Are you ill?'

She was wearing a large white apron and Swedish clogs, also white. Even her face was white, as if floured. Perhaps her nurse-like appearance was reassuring because Louis was gradually recovering.

'I had a little turn. Fairs and me, you know … But what are you doing here?'

'I'm working! You've just had the vapours beside my van!'

'The *frites* van?'

'Yes! Come and say hello to Jacques. I can't get over this, it's been ages … Guess who I saw just now?'

'Who?'

'Your son, our son.'

'Fred?'

'Yes. I haven't seen him since my parents' funeral. So much for blood ties!'

For a fraction of a second, Louis could only see red as if all the other colours had disappeared, as if it was the only colour in the world.

'Come and have a glass of water. You don't look right.'

'No, no, I'm fine. But I'm with a little girl – she's over there on the roundabout.'

'Go and get her. I'll give her a waffle with lots of whipped cream on top.'

While Mylène was covering herself in cream, Jacques and Agnès insisted on giving Louis the tour of the van, as if it were a gastronomic restaurant. It was a wonderful business! The coast in the summer, the mountains in winter and all the little extras, like here. But how was he doing? Was that his daughter? Had he put on a little weight? But his grey hair suited him. Louis replied with idiotic little laughs, squashed into a corner of the van with Mylène. Jacques and Agnès continued to serve *crêpes, gaufres* and *frites*, all the while bombarding him with questions. He felt like a marionette in a cardboard puppet theatre. The people reaching over for their orders looked at him as if he were the bearded lady, just another attraction.

'We're thinking of expanding; we'd like to get another van, a bigger one like you get in Belgium. Food sells, you know. You can't go wrong.'

'That's true. I'm happy for you. Right, I'd better take the little one back to her mother. Mothers worry easily.'

Agnès rolled her eyes. 'What, now you're concerned about mothers? You really have changed. A few years ago, you'd have had to be forced to take your son to the fair.'

'Agnès ...'

'Don't worry, Jacques, Louis doesn't mind and, anyway, it's all in the past, isn't it, Louis? By the way, if you want to see your son, he's coming here about nine o'clock.'

Marion was eating an apple and flicking through the television guide. Louis was clearing the table.

'There's a documentary about Sri Lanka on France 2 at 8.30. My friend Fanchon went there last year; she thought it was amazing. I saw her photos, it—'

The tap running in the sink muffled Marion's voice. Louis couldn't decide – the fair or not the fair? Should he see his son – or not?

He could go or not go, what did it matter? It was as if there were another question behind that question, but he didn't know what it was. Since he had come home he had wrestled with that question mark like a trout on a hook, and his indecision was contaminating his every act. 'Should I do the washing up – or not? Should I take a piss – or not? Should I scratch my nose – or not?' It was maddening.

'Louis, what are you doing?'

'I'm going to the fair.'

'What?'

It had just slipped out without him having the time to think about it, as if he were a ventriloquist's dummy and another voice had spoken for him.

'I'm going to the fair on the boulevard.'

'I thought you hated fairs!'

'I thought that too.'

'But when you went with Mylène this afternoon, you discovered you actually love them?'

'Possibly. It brought back memories.'

'Memories? I didn't even know you had a past to have memories of – you never talk about it. Do you want me to come with you?'

'I'd prefer to go on my own if you don't have any objection.'

'Why would I have an objection? It's just a bit odd. You don't look like someone who's going to the fair.'

'What do I look like?'

'Like a kid who's done something wrong, or who's about to. But in any case, don't forget your keys. I'm whacked – I don't even know if I'll make it to the end of my programme.'

'I won't be late.'

Marion went upstairs. The programme started. Louis put on his coat, hesitated by Marion's bag, then opened it and took out two 500-franc notes which he crammed into his wallet. The white cat watched him the whole time until he closed the door behind him.

The night air had the same effect on him as a damp cloth on his forehead. He could breathe again. He remembered his mother's perfume, Soir de Paris, thick, blue, in a shaped glass bottle, like an enormous precious stone. She would put one drop, no more, behind each ear, when she went out in the evening with her husband. They looked good together, like a married couple in a play. Louis would have liked them to be like that every day. Unfortunately they rarely were – only for a wedding anniversary or when his father received a promotion. The rest of the time they were just ordinary mortals.

A body was a stupid thing. All it needed was food and sleep, and on it went, just like any vehicle. But who was really driving it? As Louis got nearer to his destination, the music and smells of the fair became more and more invasive, attracting him like an insect caught in the U-bend of a basin. Yet something in him slowed his steps. He had nothing more to say to Jacques and Agnès, and not much more to say to his son. He would slip him two 500-franc notes, that was all. But he could also just give them to Agnès and go home to bed.

The ephemeral town of lights and giddiness started on the other side of the boulevard. It seemed to take for ever for the lights to turn from green to red. He couldn't fathom why he was in such a hurry to get across. A group of youths beside him were horsing about hurling insults at each other. He didn't understand a word they were saying. He crossed the boulevard in their wake as if for protection.

The fair was not the same at night. Louis didn't know where he was. He had left the group of young people in front of the big wheel. Some of them wanted to go on it, some of them didn't. He wandered about looking for Agnès's van. He was dazzled, his ears assaulted by shouts and the sharp crack of rifle shots. It wasn't the nausea of this afternoon that now took hold of him, it was more like an inebriation, quite overpowering like his mother's Soir de Paris. It was only by chance that he stumbled on Agnès's van. Fred had not arrived yet. He could either wait for him there or have a go on the big wheel; a friend of Agnès's was running it. You could see the whole of Paris from there – it was fantastic. Well, why not? Normally, Louis would have categorically refused, but normally he wouldn't even have been here. And the intoxication he still felt seemed to protect him – he wasn't afraid of anything any more; he was watched over not by a guardian angel but rather by a well-muscled bodyguard. Everything seemed fun, everything sparkled, everything seemed appealing. He felt honoured and behaved accordingly, interested by everything around him. He settled down in the gondola of the big wheel like a king, arms ready to bless the crowd. He rose. The wind was stronger, colder. Soon the fair was nothing but a stream of lava running between the trees. The gondola swayed gently each time the wheel stopped. The sky seemed closer than the ground. 'I have never been more alone. And curiously, it doesn't bother me at all. I'm not frightened of solitude any more because I'm the only one who counts, because the others don't exist, they're only there for effect.' In the gondola in front, actually below, the young man had succeeded in kissing the girl. Their kiss must have tasted of soda. They were snuggled into each other. They could have been anywhere. But they were here. A gust of wind blew the girl's scarf off. She gave a cry, putting her hand on her hair. They both burst out laughing.

Everyone on the roundabout watched the zigzagging flight of the red scarf.

The exit led him down another path, behind the big wheel, opposite a tombola festooned with blue monkey cuddly toys. Louis had an urgent need to piss, which had come over him on the last turn of the wheel. He had to get behind the stalls in order to find a suitably dark spot. The urgency of the situation made him immediately dart between two stalls. A profound ecstasy spread through him as he relieved himself against the wooden fence. 'I'm exactly where I should be; I could only be here. I can almost say I recognise this place, as clearly as if someone had described it to me a fraction of a second before I got here. Someone is guiding my actions, imperceptibly anticipating them. I am a proxy for somebody else.'

A violent shove in the back propelled him against the rough planks he was pissing against. His teeth, lips and nose all split against the wood. Without understanding how, he was on the ground. Blows rained down on his body. He tried to protect himself, one hand on his head, the other on his penis which was still outside his flies. There were several people hitting him. He could only see their legs and feet, which seemed to increase in number as the pain worsened. The toe of a boot sliced off his ear, the music from the nearest merry-go-round rushed into the wound and bored into his brain. Hands were turning him over, rootling in his pockets. No one was watching over him any more. Between half-closed eyes he could make out two figures in a ray of green light.

'A thousand big ones.'

'Toss the wallet.'

'Wait ... I want to know what this bastard's name is ...'

'Chuck it, Fred, and let's get out of here!'

'Yeah, yeah, I actually don't give a shit who he is.'

Louis's wallet landed right beside his head. The two figures disappeared round the corner of the stall. Louis could no longer move. The machine was out of order. He was in pain but that wasn't what worried him, it was the pocket of ink that had just exploded in his stomach and was filling him with night. 'I'm leaking, gently deflating ... I'm dying ... I went to the fair with a little girl called Mylène and as a result, I'm dying ... right here in the grass ...'

Close by two dogs were copulating conscientiously. They stopped for an instant, when a gurgle escaped the mouth of the man stretched out near the dustbins, then they resumed, their tongues hanging out, gazing at the moon.

21

There. Louis's back in his ink pot. I turn off the typewriter, put down my glasses, rub the sides of my nose, pick up a cigarette but don't light it. I hold the manuscript in my hand, reassured by the weight of the thing. Because this story has become a thing, a matter of so many grams. I thought Louis was going to unmask me when he said, 'Someone is guiding my actions ...' He could have slipped away from me, away from himself. I can hear Hélène moving furniture around downstairs. She told me she was going to give the place a big clean-up this morning. Hélène always does as she says.

I only stopped rolling through the grass when I touched the wheel of the car. I lay there, flat on my stomach, for a long while, filling my lungs with the smell of petrol and the warm engine, and then I lifted my head. It was light, only just, but enough to establish that Christophe was no longer standing on the edge of the cliff. I shouted his name twice, three times, simply because that's what you do in those situations, but I had already realised what had happened. I knew exactly what I would see if I peered over the edge: a body lying broken on the rocks like an old alarm clock, a body that wasn't mine. The whooshing of air I had sensed as I threw myself backwards had been Christophe being sucked into the void. My moving backwards must have thrown him off balance and …

Sitting there on the grass open-mouthed, the enormous consequences of my panic struck me full in the face. The sky had been reduced to one huge zero, round and smooth. I think I stammered, 'It wasn't me,' or else, 'It wasn't my fault.' Then fear, or an instinct of self-preservation – whatever you want to call it – took over. I didn't even check to make sure that Christophe really was at the foot of the cliff – what would have been the point? I was about to take the car, but once I got behind the wheel, I reconsidered. Why complicate the simplest of stories? 'A man in a state of shock over the death of his wife kills his mother-in-law and goes to the coast to commit suicide.'

A few lines in the local paper, no more. I wiped down the steering wheel, the bottles, the seats, the handle of my door. I walked to the village like an automaton, seeing nothing, feeling nothing, my legs stiff, the wind in my back. I waited there a good hour and a half for the bus to come. There was a café open – I could have gone in for a coffee but I didn't. I felt as conspicuous as if I was painted red. I got on the bus without thinking. A girl came and sat next to me. I could hear the *bzzzz*

bzzzz of her Walkman right in my ear. She moved her left foot to the beat, oblivious to the fact her knee was rubbing against mine. She must have taken me for a suitcase, some package or other. I moved my leg. Snatches of the night's events came prowling around me; I waved them away like mosquitoes, sent them back one by one to the chaos they had emerged from. Later, tomorrow, but not now. The road hugged the coastline. I remembered those maps of France printed on transparent plastic; you had to trace the contours with the tip of a pencil: the receding hairline of Pas-de-Calais, the frowning eye of the Seine estuary, the wart of Cherbourg on the nose of Finistère, the pout of Gironde and the pointy chin of the Landes. I could have stayed on this bus all the way to Saint-Jean-de-Luz and never taken my eyes off the coast.

I got off at the church with tears in my eyes, my nerves and muscles tight as the strings of an instrument. It was market day. The man I get my eggs and cheese from waved at me. I didn't stop. Nothing could have prevented me getting home. Having reached my front door, for one awful moment I couldn't find my keys. They had fallen inside the lining of my jacket. The first thing I did was clear the table of the previous day's leftovers, the paper the brawn had been wrapped in, the empty bottles and wine-stained glasses, the end crust of bread. I washed everything. Then I changed the sheets on the bed Christophe had slept in. I didn't want any trace of him left anywhere. Afterwards I took a shower and got changed. I went and tidied my study. I sat down in front of my typewriter and slipped a blank sheet into the carriage. There, nothing had happened; I had just got up and everything was fine and dandy. After a minute of staring like an idiot at the piece of paper, I began to feel dizzy. I filled in the empty space by typing meaningless words, among which AZERTYUIOP came up often. I had to do something, anything, to escape the silence and stillness. I threw words onto paper like twigs onto a fire, to avoid freezing on the spot; two, three, four pages of pretending to write until I heard a knock at my door. I slid behind the curtain to see who it was. I immediately recognised the Vidals' daughter, the game-show champion. Beyond her, an ambulance was parked in the road behind a beige Renault 4. The girl tried again, took a couple of steps back to peer into my window. I stayed still; she shrugged, turned and left. Two male nurses emerged from the Vidals' place carrying a stretcher on which a body lay entirely covered by a grey blanket. They slid it into the back of the ambulance the way a baker slips a batch of bread into the oven. Madame Vidal appeared, clutching her daughter's arm, her face buried in a handkerchief. One of the nurses helped her into the ambulance while her daughter struggled to lock the gate. The ambulance drove off and the girl got into the Renault. I let the curtain fall back into place.

Hélène is humming to herself while she does the hoovering. She's happy to be here, to be doing the housework, to know that I'm in the study upstairs. She and Nat made up over the phone. They'll see each other back in Paris. She thinks I was right to persuade Christophe to go and hand himself in to the police; it was the sensible thing to do. As for my neighbour's death, it's sad but, at that age, it's only to be expected at some time or another … In short, as far as she's concerned, everything is back to normal, only she doesn't think I'm looking great. A week from now she'll have me right as rain, I can count on her. What she would like more than anything is for me to be done with that damned book. She hates it without having read it; when it's off my hands, we'll go to England, or somewhere else.

And the lake's skin will heal over without a scar.